"The Bloodline Wars" Book One:

This Crown Ain't Free

(The Rise of the Survivors & Scars)

By GJ Greene

First Edition

The Bloodline Wars: This Crown Ain't Free

Written by GJ Greene

ISBN: 979-8-234-07445-4

Published by GJ Greene

Printed in the United States of America

DEDICATION

To all the creative thinkers—
the ones who dream beyond what they can see, who build worlds from scars, silence, and imagination. This story is for you.

To Melissa, my love—
you are my muse, my peace, and the quiet strength behind every page. Thank you for believing in me, even when the road felt long. Your love gave breath to this journey.

I am a fan of creation. Of genuine content. Of stories that mean something.

This one was written with heart.

TABLE OF CONTENTS

PROLOGUE

Duschinni Beach, Florida August 2004

The ocean did not care who you were.

Not your name.

Not your past.

Not your pain.

It swallowed everything the same.

The water crashed violently against Theodore Parker's body as another wave dragged him beneath the surface. Salt filled his mouth. Darkness wrapped around him like cold hands pulling him somewhere deeper than the ocean floor.

Somewhere quieter.

Above him, thunder groaned across the night sky. Lightning flashed in violent streaks over Duschinni Beach, illuminating the shoreline for half a second before the world vanished back

into blackness.

Theodore's arms moved weakly.

Too weakly.

His lungs burned.

His body felt heavy.

He opened his eyes underwater and saw nothing but distortion. Fragments. Broken pieces of light dancing through the current.

Then came the memories.

Charlotte screaming.

A shattered plate against a wall.

The sound of his own stutter trapped in his throat while laughter echoed around him.

"You'll never survive this world acting
weak."

Theodore tried to fight upward.

The ocean pulled him back down.

His chest tightened harder.

Maybe this was it.

Maybe some people were born to drown
long before they ever touched water.

Another flash of lightning cracked
across the sky.
Above the storm, the city lights of
Duschinni Beach glowed in the distance like gold
scattered across the coastline.
Beautiful from far away. Rotten underneath.

A city filled with smiling politicians,
buried secrets, old bloodlines, and people pretending
monsters only existed in stories.

But monsters were real.

Sometimes they wore suits.

Sometimes they wore crowns.

And sometimes…

They looked exactly like broken little boys trying to survive long enough to become men.

Then everything went black.
Far above the storm…
Duschinni Beach kept breathing.
Like it always did.

CHAPTER ONE: THE QUIET BELOW

The water was quiet.

Too quiet.

Theodore Parker thrashed beneath the surface, arms flailing in a panic, but his movements were sluggish, like trying to swim through syrup. His lungs screamed for air. The sun above, refracted by the waves, looked like a distant, mocking eye. His ears pulsed with pressure, each heartbeat hammering a countdown he couldn't stop.

He didn't remember falling in. One second, he'd been walking along the edge of the pier on his lunch break—headphones in, thoughts miles away—and the next, cold darkness swallowed him whole. His khakis ballooned uselessly around his legs. His button-up shirt clung like a wet straitjacket.

No one saw him.

No one heard him.

The world above carried on, oblivious to the man drowning just a few feet below the surface.

A flash of a memory pierced through the panic—his mother, Charlotte, standing over him as a child, arms crossed.

"Don’t cry, Theodore. No one’s coming to save you."

His vision dimmed at the edges. He kicked again, weakly, clawing upward. Just one breath. One.

Then—fingers broke the surface. A gasp. Cold air tore into his chest.

And then—hands. Soft but strong, wrapping around his arms, yanking him up from the water like a ghost from the deep.

Theodore coughed, sputtered, clung to the dock—but the figure was already moving. A woman. A blur in a hoodie and jeans, soaked sleeves, dark hair tied back. She disappeared into the crowd before he could even thank her.

But he knew.

It was her.

He hadn't seen her in years, not since college. Not since the long nights of cramming in the library and quiet walks back to their dorms, brushing their shoulders in silence. Not since the glances that lingered too long, the laughter that felt too easy, and the moment he almost told her how he felt—almost.

Her name was Alessia.

Back then, he hadn't been ready. Life was loud, and he was quiet. She moved like a melody, and he lived inside pauses.

And yet here she was again. Pulling him from drowning. Vanishing into the world like a phantom just when he needed saving most.

Theodore pulled himself onto the dock with trembling arms. He sat there for a full minute, drenched and shivering, coughing up pieces of whatever self-respect he had left.

He was twenty-two years old. And somehow, that moment—the quiet beneath the water—felt more honest than anything he'd experienced in years.

As Theodore sat up, still dripping, he spotted Marcus and Andrew jogging over, grins plastered across their faces.

“Man, you sure know how to make an entrance,” Marcus chuckled, clapping him on the shoulder.

Andrew smirked. “Yeah, if you wanted Alessia’s attention, there are easier ways, bro.”

Theodore couldn't help but laugh, shaking his head. “Trust me, that wasn’t part of the plan.”

Marcus leaned back, glancing at the crowd. “Speaking of making an impression, did you hear Adonis Perry’s running for mayor?”

Andrew nodded. “Yeah, it’s all anyone’s talking about. The guy’s got some serious backing.”

Theodore’s interest piqued. He listened as his friends discussed the upcoming election. Little did he know this election would soon intertwine with his own journey.

CHAPTER TWO: THE CAFÉ SHIFT

It was just past 9 p.m. on a Tuesday night when Theodore finally returned to his apartment, still damp from the pier incident hours earlier. He had dried off the best he could with the emergency towel he kept in his trunk, but the chill from the water hadn't entirely left him. Neither had the image of Alessia—emerging like a phantom, saving him without a word, and disappearing before he could even say thank you.

The apartment greeted him the way it always did with silence. Not the peaceful kind of quiet, but the hollow, echoing kind that seeped into the bones. The place was clean, almost too clean, books lined up perfectly on the shelf, dishes dried and stacked, couch cushions never out of place. It wasn't a home so much as a hideout, a bunker from the outside world.

He dropped his keys in the bowl by the door, peeled off his damp socks, and sank into the couch. The events of the day played back in his head like a reel of film stuck on repeat—Alessia's face, the weight of her hands pulling him up, the rush of cold air, and the embarrassment that clung to him more tightly than the water.

He moved through his routines with mechanical stillness. A hot shower. An oversized hoodie. Tea instead of coffee—something about the ritual helped him wind down. But the apartment still felt sterile, untouched by life.

Theodore's bedroom resembled a museum of someone else's past. The framed diploma on the wall—Business Administration, Summa Cum Laude—felt like a relic. The bookshelf held dusty self-help titles he never finished. And on the nightstand sat a photo of him and his mother, Charlotte, from high school graduation. Her hand clutched his shoulder like a vice.

He stared at that photo longer than he meant to.

"Don't cry, Theodore. No one's coming to save you."

The words still rang in his ears, years later. Her voice wasn't loud, but it was permanent.

He crawled into bed but didn't sleep right away. His mind stayed restless, tangled in old regrets and fresh confusion. Alessia's face haunted the darkness behind his eyelids.

By the next day, the sun had returned, and the city moved on like it always did. The midday light filtered through the large front windows of Margo's Café, casting warm, dappled beams across the table where Theodore sat with his two closest friends. A half-drunk coffee cooled by his elbow, untouched.

Andrew, ever the adrenaline junkie, was animated and loud, still in uniform from his paramedic shift. His sleeves were rolled, exposing arms covered in minor bruises and a tattoo of a heart wrapped in flame. Across from him sat Marcus, steady and clean-cut in his business-casual attire, his phone always within reach, his expression always calm.

Theodore said nothing. Just stirred his coffee in slow, lazy circles. The water still clung to his skin in his memory.

"So," Andrew said, tossing a sugar packet onto the table, "you should've seen this guy today—OD'd in a Wendy's drive-thru, pants down, screaming about aliens stealing his kidneys. I live for this chaos, man."

Marcus smirked. "Sounds like another Tuesday for you."

Andrew leaned back, grinning. "Damn right it is."

Theodore forced a smile. "Yeah… sounds exciting."

“Exciting?” Andrew scoffed. “Try chaotic. But that’s the juice. You gotta feel alive, you know?”

Theodore nodded, barely.

Marcus looked up from his sandwich. “Meanwhile, I spent five hours in a meeting that should’ve been an email. But hey, no blood, no screaming. Win-win.”

Theodore didn’t respond. His fingers curled tighter around the ceramic mug.

“You good, man?” Marcus asked, brows furrowing.

Theodore looked up slowly, realizing they’d noticed.

“Yeah. Just tired, I guess.”

Andrew tilted his head. “Tired or fed up?”

Theodore hesitated. He wasn’t sure which one it was anymore. Maybe both.

“My boss made a point to humiliate me in front of everyone again today,” he said. “Corrected me on something that wasn’t even wrong. Just had to flex his authority.”

Marcus frowned. "Man, you've been saying that for months. Why don't you walk?"

Andrew nodded. "For real. You've got a degree. You're smarter than that clown. What are you still doing there?"

"I don't know," Theodore muttered. "I guess… I'm not built like you guys. You both have direction. I'm still figuring out where I fit."

Andrew leaned in, his expression sharpening. "Bro. No one hands you a permission slip to live your life. You either take control, or you get dragged."

Theodore looked down at the swirl of cream in his coffee.

"I'm just tired of being the guy watching life pass him by."

There was a pause—real, heavy, not awkward.

Marcus spoke softly. "Then maybe it's time to stop watching."

Outside the window, a bird landed on the sidewalk. Still. Calm. Theodore watched it, wondering what it would feel like to simply take off.

CHAPTER THREE: GHOSTS IN THE STACKS

Flashback: The library at Danforth University always smelled like old paper and overachieving. Towering bookshelves boxed students in like academic prisons, and the overhead lights buzzed just enough to irritate but never enough to justify leaving. Theodore Parker had a favorite corner in the back, near the tall windows overlooking the north lawn. No one bothered him there.

Except her.

Alessia Tolliver had a way of showing up like a breeze through an open window—soft, unexpected, and impossible to ignore. She wasn't loud, never overbearing, but there was something electric about her presence. Like the way she hummed to herself when she studied or the way she tapped her pen when she was deep in thought. It wasn't distracting. It was grounding.

He first noticed her during sophomore year. She always chose the same table, just two rows down. Over time, their silent proximity turned into passing glances, and then into casual greetings. Eventually, she started joining him without asking, plopping her books down with a smile like she belonged there. And honestly, she did.

One night in late October, with finals creeping closer and nerves running high, Alessia looked up from her textbook and asked, "Do you ever think too much?"

Theodore blinked. "I-I-I… y-yeah. P-p-pretty much all the time."

She tilted her head. "See? That right there."

He stiffened. "W-what?"

She smiled. "Your stutter. I like it."

The words hit him like a slap he didn't expect. Kind, but jarring.

"You… l-like it?"

Alessia nodded, unbothered. "Yeah. It's yours. It's like a signature. Everyone's got something. Yours is just... audible."

Theodore looked down at his notes, face burning. He didn't know what to say to that. Every teacher, every presentation, every cruel nickname from his childhood had made that stutter feel like a curse he couldn't shake. But she wore her acceptance like it was obvious. Like it wasn't even up for debate.

"I-I d-d-don't… like it," he muttered.

"I know," she said gently. "But maybe one day you will."

They didn't speak for a few moments after that, but it wasn't awkward. It was just full. Her words sat in the space between them like a lamp in a dark room.

Later that night, as they packed up their books, Alessia dropped her highlighter and it rolled under the table. She bent to grab it, then bumped her head on the way back up. "Ow—damn," she winced.

Without thinking, Theodore reached out and tucked a loose strand of her hair behind her ear.

She froze.

So did he.

Her eyes met his, wide and open. And for a split second, he thought he saw the future in them. His mouth opened, words building in his throat, something he'd held back for weeks—

But the moment cracked. Someone slammed a book shut nearby, and the spell broke. Theodore stepped back.

Alessia gave a soft smile, then slung her backpack over her shoulder.

“See you tomorrow?” she asked.

He nodded. “Y-yeah.”

But he didn’t show up the next day.

And now, years later, she had pulled him from the water like it was nothing. Like time hadn’t moved at all.

Back then, she had seen something worth saving. And somehow, she still did.

Theodore didn’t know what terrified him more—the memory of almost drowning, or the truth that maybe he’d never really stopped holding his breath.

CHAPTER FOUR: THE ACCIDENTAL CANDIDATE

The city was buzzing. Billboards, campaign flyers, podcast ads—PERRY 4 THE PEOPLE was plastered everywhere. Adonis Perry, clean-cut and charismatic, was dominating the race for mayor. With his polished speeches and carefully curated image, he was becoming a household name. His slogan oozed populist charm, but behind the scenes, whispers of elitism and entitlement stirred among the voters. The fact that he came from money and carried the quiet arrogance of someone who never truly had to struggle only amplified the unease.

Adonis had been raised under the sharp eye of his father, Julian Perry—a corporate juggernaut who believed success wasn't earned, it was expected. Julian didn't speak in encouragements; he delivered ultimatums. "Be the best or be forgotten," he once told Adonis before a high school debate tournament. That tone never changed. Missing from the picture was Adonis's mother—a ghostly absence in his life that no achievement ever seemed to fill. Her identity was never spoken about in public, and Adonis never spoke about her in private.

This created something cold in him. Precise. Ruthless. He didn't just want to win—he had to. It was the only language he knew. Failure wasn't an option because love had always been conditional, a reward for success.

Across the aisle stood Olivia Schumacher—a native of Duschinni Beach, once the quiet, acne-riddled girl who sat in the back of every class. Now thirty-nine, she had transformed into a sharp, confident, and undeniably beautiful woman. Light brown skin, 5'6", and dressed like politics were her runway, Olivia wasn't just a contender—she was a storm. Her grassroots campaign had gained real momentum, shaking the establishment with every articulate blow. A master of strategy and public engagement, Olivia knew how to speak directly to the people—and more importantly, how to listen.

And somewhere in the eye of this political storm... was Theodore Parker.

It hadn't started with ambition. It had started with a question.

At a small neighborhood forum designed to showcase local business leaders and community thinkers, Theodore had been asked to sit on a panel. His friend Marcus—ever the networker—had thrown his name into the mix at the last minute. "You've got ideas, man," he'd said. "Real ones. People need to hear them."

The forum wasn't large—maybe thirty people seated in folding chairs in a community center—but the conversation turned unexpectedly serious. A small business owner asked what the city could do to protect their space from being bulldozed for luxury condos. Another raised concerns about education funding. Then someone asked a loaded question:

"If you were mayor, what would you do differently?"

All eyes turned to Theodore.

He could have passed. Could have deferred. But something in him stirred.

He cleared his throat, and the familiar tremor of his stutter was there—but so was the discipline he'd been working on in silence. Controlled breathing. Grounded presence.

"I-I'd st-start," he said, voice steadying as he spoke, "by l-l-listening more than talking. People d-don't need a hero. They need... someone who remembers what it feels like to b-b-be unheard."

The room stilled. Then it erupted in quiet applause. Not wild, not explosive—but genuine.

What followed was unexpected. A local blogger wrote about the event, quoting Theodore's answer word for word. A video clip made it to a small political podcast. The phrase "man of tomorrow" was plucked from another part of his speech, where Theodore had quoted a bit of philosophical reflection from his college days—"The man of tomorrow must be forged by the trials of today."

The slogan stuck.

MAN OF TOMORROW.

Soon after, a petition began circulating online urging Theodore to run. It started as a symbolic gesture. Then it gathered thousands of signatures. Marcus showed him the numbers over coffee one morning.

"You've struck a nerve, Theo. People are tired of performances. You gave them something that felt real."

"But I'm not a politician," Theodore protested.

"No," Marcus said. "You're better. You're a philosopher with something to say."

It wasn't just the stutter he was learning to control. It was the self-doubt. The fear. The belief that his voice didn't matter.

And then there was Alessia Tolliver.

In the crowd, always observing, never pushing. Her presence was quiet encouragement. She reminded him, with every glance, that he had been seen long before anyone was watching. Raised by two loving parents who taught her how to listen with her heart as much as with her ears, Alessia understood people—especially the broken parts they tried to hide. She had her own wounds. An older brother lost to addiction. A history of loving people who didn't know how to love themselves.

Still, she remained magnetic—not because she tried to be, but because she never needed to. Intelligent, intuitive, and emotionally fluent, Alessia had a way of disarming the toughest souls.

And maybe that's why, despite everything, she found herself intrigued by Adonis Perry.

She had seen him at events—rigid, ambitious, smiling like a man who practiced it in the mirror. She saw through it.

She recognized the telltale signs of a boy who had never been nurtured. Who was raised on expectations instead of affection. She didn't trust him, but she understood him.

Now, Theodore Parker stood at the edge of a path he never meant to walk. Caught between the machine-polished charm of Adonis and the sharp political fire of Olivia Schumacher, he wasn't the likely choice.

But maybe that's exactly why people were starting to believe in him.

The race wasn't just political. It was philosophical. A battle of identities, ideals, and what kind of future the city wanted to believe in.

And for the first time in his life, Theodore wasn't running away.

He was running toward it—as the man of tomorrow.

CHAPTER FIVE: SHADOWS AND SECRETS

Adonis Perry sat alone in his penthouse office, the skyline stretching behind him like a kingdom under surveillance. The walls were lined with accolades—debate championships, political science awards, commendations from boardrooms and benefactors. But tonight, they looked like trophies in a museum he didn't belong to.

He stared at the glowing laptop screen in front of him. It played Theodore Parker's now-viral town hall clip on loop. The stutter, the resolve, the applause. The crowd didn't see weakness. They saw *honesty.*

Adonis clenched his jaw. He was never taught to admire vulnerability. He was taught to annihilate it.

"Find out who this Parker guy really is," Adonis had instructed his fixer earlier that day. A man named Caldon—ex-military, now operating in the gray space where money and secrets traded hands. "Family, finances, therapy records. Dig deep. I want leverage, not headlines."

That was hours ago. Now, Caldon's encrypted report sat in his inbox. Adonis clicked.

Subject: Theodore Parker

Born: Same hospital, same year, same day... same *time*. Uncanny.

Caldon's notes were clinical, but thorough. Academic records, medical history, social connections. The section marked "Paternity" had been heavily redacted.

RECORD SEALED BY COURT ORDER

Adonis frowned. "Why would hospital birth records from over thirty years ago be redacted?"

He clicked deeper. Cross-referencing surnames, birth dates, timelines. Julian Perry had been in that city the same year Theodore was born. The math lined up. The probability was unsettling.

"Impossible," he muttered. "He would've told me."

But would he?

Julian had always spoken of legacy in the singular—*you*, not *you and your brother*. There was no room for anyone else in Julian Perry's world. If Theodore was connected by blood… he would be competition, not family.

Adonis slammed the laptop shut.

He ran a hand through his perfectly styled hair, the mask cracking just a little. For the first time in years, he felt the edge of fear. Not panic. Not dread. Just something… unfamiliar. A sliver of uncertainty.

He couldn't let it grow.

He pressed the intercom button on his desk. "Sandra, contact General Duschinni Hospital. See if you can get any archived records on a Theodore Parker. Cross-reference with the birth year 1972. Use my discretionary code. I want it quiet."

"Yes, sir," came the reply.

Adonis turned back toward the skyline, a dark smile curling at the corner of his mouth.

"Let's see how clean this man of tomorrow really is."

***

Across the city, Alessia Tolliver sat with her best friend Maribel on a rooftop balcony, sipping wine under café lights strung across the brick walls.

"He's different now," Alessia said quietly.

"Who, Theo or Adonis?" Maribel asked.

"Both," she replied. "Theo's starting to believe in himself. And Adonis… he's unraveling in slow motion, even if no one else can see it."

Maribel raised an eyebrow. "You sound like you still feel for Adonis."

"I don't *feel* for him," Alessia said, swirling her glass. "I *see* him. He doesn't know how to receive love because he never had it—at least not the way a mother gives it."

Her voice caught. "That kind of absence… it twists you. Dave had that too."

Maribel sat up straighter. "Wait. You think Adonis had something to do with Dave?"

Alessia hesitated.

"There was a guy… around the time Dave started slipping. He called himself 'D'. Real smooth. Connected. Slipping cash to people at parties, buying influence. I never saw his face clearly, but…"

"But?"

"I think it was Adonis. Or someone working for him. I don't know. But every time I look at him now, something in my gut says he knows more than he lets on."

Silence fell between them. City sounds drifted up from the street below. Alessia stared off into the night.

"If he *is* involved, I'll find out. And if he's not, I'll still know what he's capable of."

She stood and grabbed her bag. "I need to get home. Big day tomorrow. Early shift at the hospital."

"Another board meeting?" Maribel asked.

Alessia nodded. "Admin review. If anyone pulls records on Theo, it'll come across my desk."

***

Back in his office, Adonis stood at the window, fists clenched behind his back.

"Man of Tomorrow," he muttered. "Not if I erase him today."

But a voice inside—faint, fragile, buried—whispered something else.

What if he's the man you were supposed to be?

Meanwhile, just after midnight, in a small jazz bar off Oak Street, Theodore Parker clinked his glass against Marcus's and Andrew's. The mood was light. For once, he wasn't overthinking.

"To thirty days out," Marcus said, raising his bourbon. "September 1st is coming fast."

Andrew grinned. "You know what's wild? I actually think you're gonna win this thing."

Theodore smiled, the moment still surreal. "Let's just say... I'm starting to believe it too."

They laughed, joked, and let the world blur for a few hours.

Outside, campaign posters flapped in the breeze like flags in a coming war.

Election Day: **September 1, 2004.**

The countdown had begun.

CHAPTER SIX: TIDES AND TENSIONS

Three days after the rooftop jazz bar celebration, the city was easing into the final stretch of August. It was a Saturday—warm, breezy, and lazy in the way only late summer could be. Down by the boardwalk near Duschinni Beach, food trucks lined the pavement in colorful rows, each one pumping out music, aromas, and the casual chaos of a weekend crowd.

Andrew had dragged Marcus out for what he called "a little vibe reset."

"You've been uptight since that toast," Andrew said, biting into a massive Cuban sandwich.

"I'm never uptight," Marcus replied, frowning at his overpriced poke bowl. "I'm composed."

"You're constipated with khakis," Andrew shot back, laughing.

They stood in line at a taco truck when it happened. Olivia Schumacher—yes, *that* Olivia—stepped into line behind them, dressed in a breezy linen jumpsuit, oversized sunglasses, and confidence like it was stitched into her DNA.

Marcus caught her first, blinking twice to be sure.

“Well, well, well,” he said, nudging Andrew. “Look what the polls dragged in.”

Andrew turned and let out a low whistle. “Olivia Schumacher. If I knew politicians looked like this, I’d have run for city council last year.”

She smiled, lowering her sunglasses slightly. “I hope you two gentlemen aren’t always this charming in public. Or are you just this brave around tacos?”

Marcus stepped forward, hand extended. “Marcus. Financial consultant and future footnote in your memoir.”

Andrew smirked. “Andrew. Paramedic. Lover of late-night burritos and women with opinions.”

Olivia chuckled. “That’s oddly specific. And bold.”

“I find directness saves time,” Andrew said. “Like CPR, but for conversation.”

Marcus rolled his eyes. “Don’t let him fool you. He’s bold for about four minutes, and then he disappears faster than a free bar tab. I’ve seen him ghost women mid-sentence.”

Andrew narrowed his eyes. “Says the man who still brings flowers to first dates like it’s 1997.”

Marcus put a hand on his chest. “Chivalry isn’t dead. It’s just dressed better.”

Olivia laughed, genuinely entertained. “You two need a sitcom.”

“You need a drink with me,” Marcus said, confidently.

Andrew leaned in slightly. “He talks smooth, but I act. You want a man who’ll show up, not just show off.”

Marcus arched a brow. “He’s a premature ejaculator, you know.”

“Not true,” Andrew said quickly, raising his taco defensively. “That happened *once* during allergy season.”

Olivia nearly choked on her laughter. “You’re both ridiculous.”

“Which one of us is winning this debate?” Marcus asked.

She glanced between them. “I’ll let you stew on it.”

Andrew grinned. “I don’t stew. I simmer. Low and slow.”

After they grabbed their food, Olivia lingered a bit, leaning against the boardwalk rail. The ocean breeze tousled her hair as she asked, “So what’s the deal with your friend Theodore? The quiet one running for mayor?”

Marcus answered first. “Smart. Crazy smart. Policy guy, real thinker. Philosophical type, if you’re into that.”

Andrew added, “Big heart. Bit of a tortured soul thing going on. The stutter’s real, but it’s part of his charm.”

She nodded, intrigued. “Did he always want to run?”

“Not even close,” Marcus said. “He sort of got pulled into it. Like the city noticed him before he noticed himself.”

“Interesting,” Olivia murmured, mostly to herself.

She checked her watch. “I’ve got a meeting with a campaign advisor in an hour. You two made that way more entertaining than it had any right to be.”

She looked at Andrew. “I do like a man in uniform.”

Andrew's eyes lit up. "I've got three. Want to see which one's lucky?"

She walked off with a laugh and a wave. Marcus watched her go, then sighed dramatically.

"She's choosing you, isn't she?"

Andrew shrugged, grinning. "You had the better pickup line. I had the better jawline."

Marcus took a long bite of his poke. "You're still a premature ejaculator."

"Tell that to my exes."

They both laughed, the city humming around them. Somewhere in the background, posters for all three candidates fluttered on a bulletin board—Theodore Parker's freshly printed face among them.

The game was on. And even love, apparently, was up for election.

CHAPTER SEVEN: THE QUIET FALL

The night air was soft with a warm breeze as Maribel stepped out of the wine bar near the hospital. The sidewalks were quiet, the glow of streetlamps stretching long across the pavement. She had stayed a little later than planned, texting Alessia to let her know she'd be home soon. She smiled at the memory of their earlier rooftop laughter, still feeling the warmth of the evening in her chest.

Her heels clicked softly as she crossed the street toward the hospital's rear parking structure, where her car was tucked away in the lower level. She walked with confidence—Maribel was the type who didn't scare easily. Not with a sharp tongue like hers and a few years of knowing exactly how to read a room. But tonight… something felt off.

She paused as she stepped into the stairwell, her hand resting on the cool rail. It was too quiet. The kind of quiet that felt rehearsed.

She turned to head back up—

A hand, gloved and black, wrapped swiftly around her neck.

Maribel gasped, her feet lifting off the ground as her back slammed against the stairwell wall. Panic exploded in her chest. She kicked wildly, arms flailing, nails scratching leather.

The grip didn't loosen.

Her eyes bulged, blood vessels rupturing. Her lips turned a sickening shade of purple as she tried to scream, but no sound escaped.

A warm trickle ran down her thigh as she lost control of her bladder. Her shoes fell from her feet as she twisted, face contorting in silent agony.

She clawed at the arm holding her up, but the strength behind it didn't waver. It was efficient. Cold.

Her vision blurred.

She felt a breath—someone whispering.

"You should've stayed quiet."

Then—nothing.

Her arms slowly dropped from their defensive position, swinging limply at her sides.

The black gloves released her.

She slumped against the wall, crumpling like a marionette whose strings had been cut.

Footsteps echoed as her killer disappeared into the darkness. No rush. No panic. Just clean exit.

Maribel's phone buzzed from where it had landed a few feet away, still lit with the last message she had typed:

"I think someone's watching me. I'll call you in 5."

But she never would.

CHAPTER EIGHT: WHAT REMAINS

The sirens shattered the early morning silence. Alessia Tolliver stood outside the hospital's south entrance, still dressed in her workout clothes, hair tied in a loose bun. She hadn't even made it inside yet when she saw the lights, the tape, the commotion at the rear parking structure. She rushed toward the chaos, heart in her throat, dread already clinging to her skin like sweat.

Andrew spotted her first.

He stepped away from the body, glancing at his partner—a younger EMT named Rico, who knew better than to say anything in a moment like this. Andrew pulled off his gloves, walked toward Alessia, and caught her by the shoulders.

"Alessia… you need to brace yourself," he said, gently but firmly.

"What?" she asked, eyes wide. "Andrew, who is it?"

His pause said everything.

"No…" she whispered.

Andrew didn't answer. He didn't have to.

She pushed past him, her feet moving on autopilot. The scene was already cordoned off, but she ducked under the tape, ignoring the voices behind her. The body lay in the shadows against the cold concrete wall.

Shoes off.

Arms limp.

Eyes red with burst capillaries.

Her heart broke before her mind caught up.

“Maribel…”

She fell to her knees, a sound escaping her chest that didn’t resemble words—only anguish. Someone tried to pull her away, but Andrew waved them off. He knelt beside her, placing a steady hand on her back.

“Don’t look at her face,” he said softly. “Remember how she laughed. Not this.”

But Alessia couldn't look away. Not yet. She felt like she had failed her twice in one night—first by letting her walk alone, and now by being too late.

Estimated time of death: August 2, 2004 – Between 2:15 and 2:45 a.m.

Hours later, in the hospital's quiet administrative wing, Alessia sat alone in her office, the lights dim. Her hands shook as she opened Maribel's employee records and personal email logs, anything that might make sense of what had just happened.

There was a flagged message in Maribel's inbox from a few days ago. Sent to herself. No subject.

"Olivia's people are in the hospital system. Someone's accessing sealed files through the backdoor. I think I know who."

Alessia stared at the screen. Her pulse skipped.

She grabbed her coat, shoved her phone in her bag, and stormed out.

That evening, the city held a community vigil for victims of recent violent crime. Theodore stood among the attendees, coat collar up against the breeze. He didn't know what to say to Alessia yet—only that he needed to be there.

She arrived late, face pale but composed. And not alone.

Adonis Perry stood next to her, offering support like he was born for it. Smooth. Steady. Photogenic even in grief.

Maribel's parents stepped forward, her mother clutching her father's arm as she addressed the small crowd. Her voice trembled but held steady.

"Our daughter had a heart as big as this city," she said. "She never met a stranger, and she never walked away from someone in pain. We thank you all for coming tonight. She would've loved this—a night of light in the darkness."

Her father added, "She always said truth mattered more than comfort. Let that guide all of us moving forward."

The crowd bowed their heads in a moment of silence. Candles flickered. Some people wept. Others stood stiff, locked in grief.

Adonis leaned closer to Alessia and whispered, "I know this is hard. But you don't have to go through it alone. Not tonight."

She turned slightly, glassy eyes. "I don't want to be alone," she whispered.

He nodded and gently slipped his hand into hers.

Theodore felt his jaw clench as he watched. His fists balled inside his coat pockets.

Andrew leaned over to him and muttered, “You gonna let that dude photobomb your whole life?”

Theodore didn’t respond. His eyes stayed locked on Alessia and Adonis.

Adonis met his gaze and held it. There was no smile this time. Just tension.

“You here to support her?” Adonis said lowly as he passed Theodore. “Or just be seen?”

Theodore didn’t flinch. “I don’t need to be seen. I’m not the one running from something.”

Adonis paused, smirked, then kept walking.

Theodore watched him go, the air between them thick with something unspoken.

The competition had already started.

Election Day: September 1, 2004 — 30 days remaining.

And the stakes had just turned deadly.

CHAPTER NINE: ECHOES IN THE DARK

The morning after the vigil, Alessia sat in the hospital chapel, a space she rarely visited. Light filtered through the stained-glass windows, bathing the empty pews in soft color. Her hands trembled as she held Maribel's phone, finally unlocked by IT. There were no new messages. No final voice memo. Just that email. And a folder she hadn't seen before.

"Dave?"

The name froze her. Inside were scanned documents, including photos and security footage snippets. One blurry image caught her breath—a man, hoodie up, leaving the rear exit of the hospital on the night of the murder. She zoomed in. His posture. His walk. A tilt of the head she couldn't unsee.

It looked like her brother.

No... it couldn't be. Dave was gone. Lost to the streets—or so she thought.

A memory slammed into her. Dave, fifteen, bruised and high, shouting at her from their front steps. "You think you can fix me? You don't even see me."

She closed the folder, swallowing the panic. She wasn't ready to believe it. Not yet.

Three days later, Alessia found herself in the downtown archives of the privately funded mental health clinic known as CrossPoint Recovery—an institution with anonymous donors and a spotless public record. But a familiar name had come up in Maribel's files: **Olivia Schumacher**.

Under the guise of hospital network review, Alessia accessed a procurement report—**dated January 12, 2001**—showing Olivia's firm had funneled discretionary funds into the Cross Point facility. Listed under "nonprofit psychological wellness partnerships," the funding trail was clean. Too clean.

She cross-referenced internal transfer logs and found a closed-case file labeled: **D. Tolliver.**

The intake notes were haunting:

Patient admitted under OD-induced psychosis. No known relatives available for contact. Emergency sponsor signed: O. Schumacher.

Procedure logs detailed the following:

- **Date of admission:** January 10, 2001 – 3:37 a.m.
- **Detox protocol initiated:** Naloxone injection and monitored sedation.
- **Psychiatric observation:** Signs of PTSD, identity distortion, dissociative episodes.
- **Mental conditioning under clinical hypnosis requested by sponsor.**

Requested. By Olivia.

Alessia's breath caught in her throat. Her fingers scrolled further through the digital report, heart hammering.

A note dated **February 2, 2001**:

Patient exhibits loyalty fixation on sponsor. Willing to engage in behavior deemed morally deviant if framed as protective toward sponsor.

She stared at the screen, paralyzed.

Olivia had manipulated him. She didn't just save Dave—she *rewrote him.*

Across the city, Theodore sat alone in his apartment, the silence feeling heavier than usual. The stress was mounting.

Media calls, smear whispers, and now Alessia pulling away.

He stood and paced, trying to push past the weight on his chest, the rising heat under his skin. Then came the shaking—the tremble in his hand, the way his jaw locked tight.

"Y-you w-w-will never be enough."

His mother's voice. Loud. Final. A whip across his memory.

Theodore stumbled to the bathroom and stared into the mirror. His eyes were glassy, unfocused.

And then something… *shifted.*

He blinked, and the man looking back at him seemed taller. Straighter. Fierce.

"Teddy," he whispered.

He hadn't said that name in years.

His therapist had once noted signs of dissociation. A fragmenting of identity under emotional distress. Teddy was everything Theodore couldn't be—cold, composed, unshakable.

His diagnosis—buried in sealed records, hidden beneath years of coping strategies—**Dissociative Identity Disorder.**

But Teddy was supposed to be gone.

Until now.

Alessia walked into the hospital's records department, barely acknowledging the staff. She used her clearance to access the restricted files.

She searched: **Parker, Theodore.**

Redacted notes. Flagged therapy summaries. Psychological observations from childhood.

Split personality episodes. Emotional detachment under duress. Hostility during suppressed trauma triggers.

Her eyes widened.

"What are you hiding, Theo…?" she whispered.

Later that night, Alessia attended a community fundraiser for the victims of citywide violence. It was less formal than the vigil—food trucks, music, political figures mingling casually. The mood was lighter, but Alessia felt none of it.

She stood near a garden lantern, arms crossed.

Adonis approached first. "I was hoping you'd come."

"I wasn't sure I would," she replied.

"I'm glad you did. You're the strongest person I've seen in all this."

"You don't know me that well," she said quietly.

Adonis tilted his head. "I know you care. About truth. About justice. That's enough for me."

Before she could respond, Theodore stepped into the circle. He looked different—composed, but distant. His eyes darker. His stance firmer.

"Alessia," he said.

She looked between them.

Adonis gave a polite nod. "Theo."

Theodore didn't return it. "We need to talk."

Alessia raised an eyebrow. "About what?"

He hesitated. "About what Maribel found. And… about me."

Adonis stepped slightly forward. "She doesn't owe you anything, Parker. Not after what she's been through."

Theodore's voice dropped. "And you do?"

Alessia held up her hand. "Enough. Both of you. I'm not a prize. I'm not a photo op. If either of you wants my time, start acting like you deserve it."

Both men stepped back. The crowd continued to buzz around them, unaware of the quiet war at the center.

Election Day: September 1, 2004 — 26 days remaining.

And the fractures were starting to show.

CHAPTER TEN: UNDERNEATH IT ALL

Date: August 8, 2004 – 7:41 a.m.

The morning broke dull and gray, a curtain of overcast skies hanging low over Duschinni Beach. Alessia sat in her car across the street from Cross Point Recovery, the building's sterile glass façade reflecting nothing but clouds. She hadn't told anyone she was coming back—not even Andrew.

Inside, she used her administrative credentials from General Duschinni Hospital to request access under a medical partnership audit. The clerk, distracted by a blinking monitor and the scent of fresh coffee, barely looked up as he buzzed her in.

Room 302, Archive Suite.

The digital files were clean. Sanitized. But Alessia knew what to look for now.

She found the second-tier records behind a hidden administrator login—logged under "Discretionary Clinical Review."

There it was:

Patient: Tolliver, David A.

Date of Extended Stay Admission: January 10, 2001 – 3:37 a.m.

Emergency Contact/Sponsor: Olivia Schumacher

Treatment notes were darker this time. More personal.

Jan 15, 2001: Patient shows post-detox recovery with paranoia symptoms. Reports nightmares of being "erased." Emergency sponsor has requested isolated therapeutic environment.

Jan 22, 2001: Initial therapeutic bonding between patient and sponsor successful. Subject begins to refer to sponsor as "guardian."

Feb 2, 2001: Hypnotherapy trial #3. Patient expresses unconditional loyalty toward sponsor. Displaying aggressive protectiveness. Recommends further moral desensitization. Subject believes sponsor saved his life after family abandonment.

Feb 17, 2001: Behavioral compliance achieved under suggestion. Patient believes removing threats to sponsor is justified.

Alessia sat back in the chair, hand trembling over the trackpad.

He wasn't just saved—he was reprogrammed.

Dave had been rebuilt into something loyal and lethal. And he truly believed Alessia had abandoned him. That Maribel had helped keep her away.

She pulled up one final document:

"Consent to Memory Regulation via Hypnotic Conditioning – Signed by Patient"

And below it—**Olivia's digital signature.**

Date: August 8, 2004 – 10:18 p.m.

Theodore stood in his living room, TV muted, the local news scrolling silently. His hands were clenched behind his back, shoulders tight.

The debate invite had come in.

Adonis, Olivia, and Theodore—live. On stage. In front of the entire city.

He stared at the envelope like it was a grenade.

Suddenly, his hand began to twitch again.

Teddy.

He paced to the bathroom and splashed cold water on his face. When he looked up into the mirror, his expression had shifted. Slight sneer. Brows lower. The boy who took beatings and never cried.

He whispered, “They want a fight... they’ll get one.”

Then the voice in his head—*not his*, but tethered to him—said:

“Let me drive, Theo. I’ll make sure they bleed.”

Alessia walked into Adonis’s apartment. He made dinner—rice, grilled chicken, broccoli, and wine. But she barely touched it.

“I found him,” she finally said.

Adonis’s fork froze. “Dave?”

She nodded. “He’s alive. And he’s been used. Olivia’s people broke him… made him into something else. Maribel figured it out. That’s why she’s gone.”

Adonis's face went cold. "Are you safe?"

"I don't know."

He reached across the table and took her hand. "Then we figure it out. We dig. Quietly. Together."

She nodded slowly, grateful—but still hollow.

"I just need to know," she whispered. "If there's anything left of the brother I loved."

Outside, thunder rumbled in the distance.

Election Day: September 1, 2004 — 23 days remaining.

And the truth was no longer buried. It was bleeding toward the surface.

CHAPTER ELEVEN: DANGEROUS CHARMS

The restaurant was upscale, tucked into the side of an old, renovated warehouse in the Duschinni Wharf district. Low lights, smooth jazz, and the scent of wood-fired cuisine filled the air. Alessia walked in wearing a short, backless crimson dress that hugged her curves with bold confidence. Her skin glowed beneath the amber lighting, and her high heels made every step echo with grace and allure. Heads turned as she passed, but she didn't notice. Her eyes were already locked on the man in the corner booth.

Adonis Perry stood as she approached. Dressed in a charcoal gray suit with the collar slightly open, his presence was magnetic. Masculine and statuesque, his deep brown eyes held just the right amount of mystery, and the way his cologne lingered in the air made her pulse skip. There was something unapologetically sensual about him—dangerous, but delicious.

"Alessia," he said, voice smooth as velvet, taking her hand and kissing the back of it with a deliberate pause. "You're breathtaking. That dress wasn't made for anyone else but you."

“You say that like you’ve rehearsed it,” she replied, her smirk hiding the way her stomach flipped.

“I didn’t have to. You walked in and stole every line I had.”

They slid into the booth, and the wine arrived—an expensive red he’d ordered in advance. He poured her a glass without breaking eye contact.

She took a sip, watching him over the rim. “So why did you really want to see me tonight?”

He leaned forward, elbows on the table, voice low and intimate. “Because I can’t stop thinking about what it feels like to be near you. And because I don’t want to pretend anymore.”

“You’re good,” she said, trying to sound unaffected. “Dangerously good.”

Adonis smiled slowly. “You ever think about what it would be like... if you stopped resisting?”

Alessia felt heat crawl up her thighs. She crossed her legs slowly, her eyes narrowing. “You want honesty?”

He nodded.

"I think about it. About you. About letting go for one night just to see how far we'd fall."

His breath hitched slightly, and he reached across the table again, this time taking her hand with more intention.

"You wouldn't fall," he murmured. "You'd burn with me."

She didn't pull away. Her fingers tangled with his, the table suddenly feeling too small.

"You're trouble," she whispered.

"I'm exactly what you've needed, Alessia."

The tension hung there like a flame between them. And then, unable to resist, he leaned in. She met him halfway, their lips brushing once… then again, deeper. Her hand slid along his jaw. It wasn't rushed. It was electric. Measured. Controlled heat.

When she finally pulled away, her breath was uneven.

"I should go," she said softly, voice barely above a whisper.

"You don't have to."

She shook her head, standing slowly. "I know. But if I stay, we'll both forget what this night was really about."

Adonis rose with her, eyes still fixed on her lips.

"Then don't forget it," he said. "Use it."

She walked away, heels clicking again, but slower, almost reluctantly.

Adonis watched her until she disappeared around the corner.

Then he reached into his coat and pulled out his phone.

"Caldon," he said into the line. "Start tailing Andrew—Theodore's boy. Discreet but thorough. I want to know if he's seen anything. Talked to anyone. And while you're at it… dig deeper into the girl who died. Maribel."

A pause.

"And one more thing," Adonis added, voice darkening. "Dave Tolliver might still be alive. If he is, I want to know who's hiding him—and who he's working for."

He ended the call and leaned back in his seat, fingers tracing the rim of his wine glass.

Election Day: September 1, 2004 — 22 days remaining.

And the web he spun was tightening around them all.

CHAPTER TWELVE: WHEN SHADOWS MOVE

The apartment was dead silent except for the hum of the refrigerator and the occasional creak of an old pipe. Theodore sat on the edge of his bed, drenched in sweat, fingers trembling.

Then it started—the flashback.

He was seven again.

Charlotte Parker towered over him, her hand clenched around a belt worn from use, her voice a knife slicing through the air.

"You little stain! You think anyone will ever want you? Speak up, boy!"

“I-I—”

“Spit it out, you pathetic stuttering freak!”

The belt cracked across his back. Once. Twice. Again. The pain was white-hot, and each lash opened skin, leaving raised, bleeding welts that would become thick, permanent scars.

"Because of you, I lost everything! Do you think your father ever wanted to raise a freak like you?" she hissed, pacing. "I could've been something. I had opportunities—modeling, travel, a life. But no. I got stuck with a mistake. With *you*."

Young Theodore screamed but covered his mouth with his hand, trained to silence his own suffering. Blood soaked through the back of his shirt. She grabbed him by the hair and yanked him toward the coat closet.

"You make one noise, and I'll forget you exist," she whispered, pushing him inside and slamming the door.

The air had gone thin in that closet. The darkness pressed against his skin like a second body. Hours passed. He wet himself. The shame became another layer of skin.

His back throbbed with fire. The lashes stung, his skin sticky with blood. The silence was unbearable—but the sound of her heels pacing back and forth outside the door was worse.

"You ruined my life," she murmured on the other side. "You'll never be anything more than the reason I failed."

That was the first time he spoke to Teddy.

In the pitch black, somewhere deep in his mind, a voice—his own, but different—whispered:

"She can't hurt us in here."

Theodore closed his eyes, trembling. "Wh-who are you?"

"I'm the one who doesn't cry. The one who doesn't stutter. I'm the part of you she can't break."

He breathed slower. The pain faded, if only slightly. The shame quieted. It wasn't comfort in the real world—but it was safety in his imagination.

That night, in a closet reeking of blood and urine, Theodore Parker began to split. Teddy was born not out of madness—but out of necessity.

Present.

Theodore's breaths came in shallow gasps. He stumbled into the bathroom, stared into the mirror—and saw someone else looking back.

Not a stranger. A shadow.

Teddy.

The sneer curled first. Then the squint. Confidence in the eyes. No fear. No trembling.

"Let me out," the reflection said.

Theodore's hand clenched the sink, knuckles white.

"No."

"You can't protect them. You can't even protect yourself."

He looked deeper into his own eyes, and for a second, he saw the same darkness from the closet.

In that place—inside his mind—he still visited Teddy. A hallway of memories, a dark room with a locked door where Teddy waited, sitting in a chair, legs crossed, smirking like he'd been expecting him.

"This is where we're safe," Teddy said.

"No," Theodore muttered to the mirror. "Not anymore."

His phone buzzed. Marcus.

"Theo, open up, man. I'm outside."

He staggered to the door and opened it slowly. Marcus took one look and froze.

“You alright?”

Theodore nodded too quickly.

“You don’t look it. You been sleepin’?”

Theodore’s voice was low. “I need to talk to Alessia.”

Marcus frowned. “You think she’s picking sides?”

“I don’t know who I can trust anymore.”

Andrew tossed a food container into a street bin outside St. Julian’s Clinic. It had been a long shift. He glanced down the block and saw a figure in a hoodie slipping into an alleyway.

He paused.

The gait. The build. Something about it tugged at him.

“Dave?” he whispered.

He followed, cautiously, weaving through the tight corridor.

Gone.

But from a parked car, Caldon watched. Camera ready. Tracker pinging.

He dialed Adonis.

"Andrew just spotted someone. Could be Dave Tolliver. Your hunch might be right."

Adonis grinned into the receiver. "Follow him. Quietly. If Dave's alive, he'll lead us to who's protecting him."

Alessia stood at her window, her phone in her hand, unread messages from Theodore stacked in her inbox. Her lips still tingled from Adonis' kiss, but her mind buzzed with confusion.

Grief clawed at her. Maribel was gone. Her brother might be a killer. And now Theodore… unraveling.

She opened a message finally:

Theo: *I need you. Please. I'm slipping.*

She closed her eyes, fingers hovering over the screen.

She didn't type anything back.

Instead, she turned off her phone and dropped it on the counter, then stood there with her hands gripping the edge of the sink.

"What am I doing?" she whispered to herself, the city lights reflecting off her tear-rimmed eyes.

Outside, across the street, in the shadows… a hooded figure watched her apartment.

Still. Silent.

Dave Tolliver was closer than any of them realized.

Election Day: September 1, 2004 — 20 days remaining.

CHAPTER THIRTEEN: THE BREAKING POINT

Date: August 14, 2004 – 3:11 p.m.

Theodore sat in a city park under the shade of an old oak, his eyes scanning the skyline, but seeing nothing. His phone buzzed in his hand—Marcus again.

"Theo, we gotta talk, man. Face-to-face. You ain't been right lately."

Theodore didn't answer. He stared into space, barely blinking.

Marcus in Theodore's Apartment – 4:02 p.m.

Marcus paced the floor, jaw tight. "You're shut down. Completely. You're fading, and I'm not just gonna stand here and watch it happen."

Theodore sat on the edge of the couch, hands on his knees, unmoving. His eyes were glassy.

"I'm fine," he muttered.

"No, you're not."

Marcus crossed the room and grabbed Theodore's shoulders. "Talk to me, bro. Say something real. Please."

Theodore flinched. Then stiffened.

And suddenly, he changed.

He stood slowly. His voice dropped.

"You're too loud."

Marcus froze. "What?"

"I said," the voice—*Teddy's* voice—repeated, "you're too loud."

Marcus took a step back. "Yo… what is this?"

Teddy looked at him, eyes narrow. Cold. Unapologetic.

"I don't like being interrupted."

Marcus blinked. "Theo?"

"No. Not right now."

Then, without warning, Theodore's hand snapped forward, gripping Marcus by the collar and slamming him against the wall. The move was fast. Controlled. Violent.

Marcus struggled. “What the hell, man?! You’re not acting like you!”

Teddy’s voice was calm. “I never said I was.”

He released Marcus, stepping back. The tension broke—but the air was different now.

Marcus looked into his friend’s face and saw something terrifying.

“You’re not… you,” he said quietly.

“No,” Teddy replied. “I’m the one who survives.”

Andrew at the hospital – 6:14 p.m.

He walked briskly through the back halls of General Duschinni Hospital, retracing steps from two nights ago. The figure he saw—the gait—it *had* to be Dave. He couldn’t let it go.

He ducked into the stairwell. Alone.

Footsteps echoed above.

Andrew froze.

Then he saw him.

Dave.

Standing at the top of the stairs. Hoodie down. Eyes locked on Andrew.

"Dave?" Andrew whispered.

Dave didn't move. But his hands trembled.

"I didn't mean to…" he muttered. "I didn't know she'd be there."

Andrew took a step up. "You're alive. We can fix this. You're not alone."

Dave's head tilted. "You shouldn't be here."

Behind Andrew, a sound—quiet, but distinct.

The door opened.

Caldon.

Camera out. Gun holstered.

"Move aside," he said to Andrew. "Now."

Andrew turned, blocking the stairwell. "He's not your target. He's family."

"I don't care if he's Santa Claus. Olivia wants him found."

Dave bolted.

Caldon shoved Andrew aside and gave chase. The hallway echoed with the sound of boots and panic.

Alessia – 7:02 p.m.

She sat in her office, the door locked, lights dim. Her hands trembled as she looked over security footage.

There he was.

Dave.

Two days ago. Near the morgue wing. Standing still. Watching. Right before Maribel died.

Her heart cracked.

A knock on the door.

It was Marcus.

"He's not okay," Marcus said. "Theo—he's not in there anymore. Something's wrong. Something *big*."

Alessia swallowed, her voice thin. "I know."

Marcus stepped forward. “He changed in front of me. It was like a whole different person. He called himself Teddy.”

Her breath caught.

“Oh my God…”

Theodore’s Apartment – 8:48 p.m.

Theodore sat on the floor of his bedroom, lights off. The shadows moved around him.

He whispered into the dark.

“I can’t stop it. I can’t hold him back.”

Teddy’s voice echoed from the walls of his mind.

“You don’t need to. Let me protect us. You were never built for war.”

Theodore clenched his eyes shut.

“I don’t want to lose myself.”

“You already did,” Teddy whispered.

CHAPTER FOURTEEN: THE EYE OF THE STORM

The sun dipped low over Duschinni Beach, casting long golden streaks across the city's rough edges. This was the quiet before the storm.

Inside General Duschinni Hospital, Alessia Tolliver sat in her office surrounded by the steady hum of admin staff, charts, and ringing phones. But her mind was far from paperwork. Her thoughts were drowning in the chaos of recent events. Dave is in critical condition. Theodore missing work. The city whispering about an unraveling candidate.

Suddenly, Detective Marcus Cain and his new partner, Detective Jasmine Moreno, entered the office. Marcus leaned on the doorway like a man already hunting ghosts.

"Ms. Tolliver, mind if we have a word?"

She nodded slowly. "Of course, Detective Cain. About Dave?"

Marcus stepped in, his voice low. "Among other things. I have questions about Theodore Parker's involvement at the hospital that night. Witness statements conflict. But you were there. What exactly happened?"

Alessia's hands tightened. "Theodore... saved my life, Detective. Whatever else people saw, that's the truth."

Marcus studied her. "That's what I needed to know. But someone out there wants that truth twisted. Be careful, Ms. Tolliver."

As they exited, Nurse Jenkins approached the front desk, muttering nervously. "Some hospital investigator asked strange questions about Mr. Parker. Real strange. Said something about Adonis Perry..."

Marcus's eyes narrowed. Moreno whispered, "That smell like Caldon to you?"

"Smells like war," Marcus replied.

Elsewhere in Duschinni Beach

Adonis Perry sat in his father's penthouse suite, stewing in quiet rage. His polling numbers were flatlined. Whispers about Theodore refused to die.

Julian Perry entered, sharply as a blade. "Adonis, take the bull by the horns. Smile for the cameras. Destroy him when it counts. Remember Law One from *the 48 Laws of*

Power—never outshine the master, unless you're ready to bury him completely."

Adonis gritted his teeth. He wasn't sure who the real master was anymore.

Back at Alessia's Office

The night wound down. Alessia gathered her things. She thought about Theodore's scars, his protectiveness... the raw man beneath the campaign chaos.

As she left the hospital, the night air hit her skin like a reminder:

Everything was about to break.

CHAPTER FIFTEEN: ASHES OF MEMORY

Flashback 1: Charlotte's Apartment – One Week Earlier

Charlotte Parker sat on a lumpy floral couch, flicking through TV channels with a cigarette balanced on her lip. The small living room was dim, the air stale, the scent of old grease and cheap perfume hanging heavy. She paused when she saw a news anchor standing in front of a campaign rally banner.

"Theodore Parker has steadily gained traction in the mayoral race..."

Her eyes narrowed as she leaned closer.

The screen showed Theodore shaking hands, smiling, answering questions. Poised. Polished. Clean cut.

Charlotte scoffed. "Look at him. Mr. Perfect. Mr. Untouchable."

She took a long drag from her cigarette and exhaled toward the screen.

"You think I don't remember you screaming for me to leave the closet door open? Crying' like a little girl. I gave up everything for you."

The anchor continued. Theodore's speech, his vision for Duschinni Beach. People cheered in the background.

Charlotte squinted. "You're still that stuttering little boy who pissed himself in my closet. Just dressed up in lies."

Her voice cracked slightly. She shifted in her seat, eyes briefly glossing over. She had raised him alone. Missed nights out. Lost jobs. Scrubbed floors while nursing bruises and bitter thoughts. She remembered the men that stopped coming around once they saw "the kid."

She remembered hunger. Rent overdue. Cold winters with no heat. Holidays skipped. And that boy—always needing, always wanting, never grateful.

"I sacrificed for you. I put my body on the line. My pride. My damn sanity. You were a leash around my neck."

But beneath the anger, envy simmered.

He was out there. Accomplished. Admired. While she was stuck in this box of faded wallpaper and broken dreams. He had risen above the life that buried her.

And he had done it without her.

The applause on the screen hit a peak. Theodore's name chanted in unison.

Charlotte's expression hardened.

"And now you think you're better than me."

She blew smoke at the screen again, slow and deliberate. "Don't forget who made you, Theo. And don't think for a second I won't unmake you."

Then, her phone rang.

Flashback 2: Charlotte's Phone Call with Olivia – That Same Night

Charlotte answered, her tone biting. "Yeah?"

The voice on the other end was smooth—unnaturally smooth. Cloaked in warmth, but beneath it, something serpentine slithered between the syllables.

"Ms. Parker," the voice said. "My name is Jennifer Langley. I'm a journalist with *The Duschinni Current*. I've been watching the election closely, and we believe it's time the *real* story of your son was told."

Charlotte's eyes narrowed. "What do you mean, 'real story'?"

The voice chuckled softly. It wasn't comforting. It was cold. Like wind drifting through a cracked window in the dead of night.

"Let's not pretend he's who they say he is, Ms. Parker. We both know better. Don't you want your voice to be heard? Don't you want people to know what *really* hides behind his polished campaign smile?"

Charlotte lit another cigarette with shaking fingers. "I've waited a long time for someone to ask me that."

"We'd like to meet. Privately. Think of it as… confession meets justice. A cleansing. You'll finally get your moment. Your truth. The spotlight you deserve."

Charlotte exhaled slowly, smoke curling through the dim kitchen air.

"When and where?"

"Tomorrow. I'll text the address. Just bring your truth."

As the call ended, Charlotte felt a chill that didn't come from the room. Something about that voice... it didn't just want her story. It wanted blood.

It wasn't Jennifer Langley.

It was Olivia Schumacher's assistant.

And it wasn't a feature. It was a summoning.

Flashback 3: Marcus – Present Day – 12:34 p.m.

Detective Marcus Cain leaned against the side of his unmarked police cruiser in the Duschinni Beach Police Department parking lot, sipping bad coffee and staring off into nothing. The five-hour meeting he'd sat through earlier that morning had left his mind spinning, but not because of paperwork or protocol.

It was what he saw in Theodore.

Then a memory surfaced. One he hadn't thought of in years.

They were thirteen. Theodore was being cornered in the middle school hallway by two boys twice his size. One of them pushed him hard into a locker.

Theodore didn't cry. Didn't beg. He looked up, dazed—and then, it happened.

His face went blank. Not scared. Not angry. *Blank.*

And when he spoke, it was low. Even.

"I said, don't touch me again."

The tone sent a chill through Marcus, even then.

Before anyone could react, Theodore lunged. He grabbed one of the bullies by the collar, slammed him into the lockers, then delivered a vicious blow to the side of the boy's head. The second kid tried to pull him off, but Theodore turned with a look so dark it made the boy freeze.

Teachers came running. Kids screamed. Blood dripped onto the floor.

Marcus had tried to grab him. "Theo! Stop, man! Stop!"

But Theodore didn't stop. Not until a teacher physically pulled him off.

Later, in the principal's office, Theodore sat silent, trembling. He didn't remember what happened. Not a second of it.

"I blacked out," he whispered to Marcus afterward. "It wasn't me."

Back then, they laughed it off. Called it "Theo's dark side."

But now, Marcus wasn't laughing.

He looked across the hall that day and remembered Andrew, standing near the nurse's office, watching everything unfold. Calm. Focused. The only one who didn't panic. Even then, Andrew had stepped in to keep the injured kid steady, grabbed tissues, kept others from crowding.

Afterward, Andrew said, "Somebody's gotta keep their cool when things go sideways."

Marcus remembered saying, "You sure you're not gonna be a doctor or something?"

Andrew shrugged. "Nah. Paramedic maybe. Somebody who gets there first."

Now, years later, it all felt connected.

He'd seen that look again. Recently.

And something else weighed on him—Detective Eugene Greene had caught the Maribel case officially, but Marcus hadn't stopped investigating. Not really. He couldn't. Not with what he knew. Not with whom he suspected might've been there that night.

His hand gripped his patrol radio instinctively.

He pulled out his phone and dialed.

"Andrew, pick up. I think I know what's wrong with him."

CHAPTER SIXTEEN: WHEN GOD LOOKED AWAY

Date: August 16, 2004 – 4:18 p.m.

General Duschinni Hospital buzzed with its usual end-of-day energy—carts clattering, shoes squeaking, nurses laughing quietly as they passed paperwork. But inside Alessia Tolliver's office, everything felt wrong. Still. The air was heavy and electric.

She stood by the window, arms crossed, staring down at the staff entrance. Her parents, Matthew and Jessica, were due at any moment. She hadn't told them what happened to Dave. Not all of it. Not yet.

A knock.

She turned, expecting her assistant.

But it wasn't.

It was Dave.

Disheveled. Pale. Eyes rang with fatigue and something else—something broken.

"Liss," he whispered, stepping in before she could react. "I need to talk to you."

Her throat tightened. “Dave… how did you get in here?”

“I didn’t mean for it to happen,” he said, rambling now. “Maribel... she wasn’t supposed to be there. Olivia told me—”

He grabbed her by the wrist.

“You told them I was dead, didn’t you?”

“Dave, please—”

“They made me a weapon, Liss. They *used me.* And now you’re just like them.”

He shoved her back—this time harder. She hit the side of her desk and let out a guttural cry.

Down the hallway, Theodore, Marcus, and Andrew were approaching. They had come to the hospital after a tense phone call from Marcus reporting unusual activity in the surveillance logs. Theodore hadn’t slept in over twenty-four hours. He knew something was coming. His bones felt it.

The moment they heard the scream; all three men sprinted toward her office.

Theodore burst through first. He froze at the sight of Dave looming over Alessia, fists clenched.

Then, it happened.

Teddy took over.

Theodore's body moved with uncanny focus. His posture was straightened. The softness in his eyes vanished.

"Let her go," Teddy said.

Dave turned. Eyes wild, confused. "Who the hell are you?"

"I'm the part of him you shouldn't test."

Dave screamed and grabbed a scalpel from Alessia's desk. He lunged.

Teddy met him mid-charge, grabbed his wrist mid-swing, and twisted. The scalpel fell. Dave screamed in pain.

Teddy slammed him against the wall. Blood splattered across the blinds. One punch. Two. A crack echoed—ribs or jaw.

Dave fought back, scratching, clawing, but Teddy was faster, sharper, and surgical.

He threw Dave across the room, his body skidding against the floor and slamming into the filing cabinet. Blood pooled near his side. He groaned, struggling to breathe.

Alessia cried out, "Stop! You're going to kill him!"

Teddy turned, panting. Rage flickering in his expression.

Then, the flicker passed. He dropped Dave's collar and stepped back.

Code blue blared.

Andrew rushed to Dave's side, already calling out procedures. "He's coding! We need a crash cart now!"

Marcus cleared the doorway for hospital staff. A gurney rolled in seconds later.

"BP's crashing—severe internal bleeding!" one nurse shouted.

"Prep him for OR—liver damage possible. He's going into shock!" another yelled.

A paramedic pushed the Ambu bag. "Bag him! He's not breathing on his own!"

Paddles were prepped. "Clear!"

Dave's body jumped. Nothing.

"Again clear!"

Beep. Beep. A slow return to rhythm.

They loaded him onto the gurney, covered in blood, a tangle of wires, tubes, and oxygen. His face was barely recognizable. Alessia sobbed as she backed against the wall.

The elevator dinged.

Matthew and Jessica Tolliver stepped out—smiling, mid-conversation—until they saw their daughter trembling, blood on her blouse, as her brother was wheeled past on the verge of death.

Jessica's face went pale. Matthew stepped protectively in front of her.

"What the hell is going on?"

Teddy turned to face them—but it was Theodore again. The mask had slipped. He looked down at his hands. Bloodied. Shaking.

"I… I don't remember."

Alessia collapsed to her knees. "He's my brother, Theo. You nearly killed my brother."

"I wasn't me," he said. "I swear to God—I wasn't me."

Later that night

In the trauma unit, Dave lay unconscious on a ventilator. Monitors beeped softly. Tubes threaded in and out of his body like vines. Nurses moved with practiced urgency. One surgeon emerged, shaking his head.

"He's stable for now. But he might not wake up."

Alessia sat beside him, her fingers curled around his. "Please don't go, Dave. Not like this."

Outside the room, Marcus reviewed footage from the hospital hallway. In the background of one shot, a nurse dropped a file.

He paused it.

Birth records. Same date. Same hospital. One marked 'Theodore Parker.' One marked 'Baby Boy - Perry.'

His eyes narrowed.

"No way," he whispered.

***

Elsewhere, in a darkened room

Olivia sat watching the footage of Dave's takedown. She smiled.

Behind her, Charlotte Parker leaned forward, microphone clipped to her collar, face painted and ready.

"You ready to go live?" Olivia asked.

Charlotte lit a cigarette. "Let's unmake him."

CHAPTER SEVENTEEN: THE HUNTERS AND THE HAUNTED

Date: August 17, 2004 – 6:12 a.m.

The sun hadn't yet broken the skyline when Caldon stepped into the hospital's ICU corridor. His coat was crisp, his walk deliberate. No one questioned him. He always had the right badge, the right tone. This morning, he posed as a hospital compliance investigator.

But he wasn't there to investigate. He was there to manipulate.

Dave Tolliver's condition had become a volatile liability, and Olivia wanted the loose ends burned. Caldon leaned in close to the ICU nurse's desk, his tone low and deliberate. "HIPAA doesn't cover conspiracies. If you saw anything… abnormal about Theodore Parker yesterday, now's the time to share it."

The nurse blinked. "Like what?"

"A man… becoming someone else."

The nurse's brow furrowed.

Caldon leaned closer, lowering his voice to a near whisper. “He changed. Right in front of everyone. One second, he was trembling. The next, he was someone else entirely. Violent. Calculated. And you—you were here. You saw it, didn’t you?”

“I—I don’t know what I saw,” she stammered.

He smirked slightly. “That’s alright. Memories are funny things. Especially under stress. But I bet you’ll remember him saying something about Adonis Perry. Maybe something like… ‘He told me to do this.’”

She looked down, visibly unsettled.

“You’re doing the right thing,” Caldon said smoothly. “The city deserves the truth. And you deserve peace.”

She paled.

Caldon walked off without another word, a phantom in motion. Moments later, he slipped into the ICU under the guise of checking equipment. No cameras caught the thin needle he inserted into Dave’s IV line—a slow-release sedative, just enough to complicate recovery.

Meanwhile, across town, Adonis stood in his father's office, the early news coverage rolling across the bottom of the television screen:

"Mayoral candidate Theodore Parker involved in violent altercation at local hospital. One man in critical condition."

Julian sipped his espresso. "You're lucky, son. The universe handed you Parker's implosion on a silver platter."

But Adonis wasn't smiling.

He had watched the footage on his own. Studied it. The way Parker moved.

"Why does he move like me?" he muttered.

Julian raised an eyebrow. "You're imagining things."

Adonis didn't answer. He couldn't shake the unease.

Julian stepped forward, voice firm, charismatic.

He glanced out the window before turning back to Adonis, eyes narrowed with the weight of a thousand calculations.

"Let me tell you something they won't teach you in any debate prep," he said. "Years ago, I had a competitor—brilliant, loud, beloved by the press. He thought charm was power. I smiled at every handshake, nodded at every insult, and waited. Until the day I exposed his affair with a donor's wife. Not by leaking it—no. By inviting them both to a charity gala and seating them next to the press corps."

Adonis raised his eyebrows.

Julian continued, a faint smirk curving his lips. "Never outshine the master, son—that's Law One from Robert Greene's *The 48 Laws of Power*. But when you *must*, make sure your shadow blinds everyone else. Crush them entirely—reputation, rhythm, resolve. Parker's unstable, but he's also dangerous. So, while he's bleeding out sympathy, you need to smile into every camera, talk about unity, talk about dignity. And the moment his mask slips again... you drive the blade in."

He sipped his espresso again. "This isn't politics, Adonis. This is war dressed in a suit. Win the crowd. Then burn the opponent when they bow. Just like Sun Tzu said in *The Art of War*—'Appear weak when you are strong, and strong when you are weak.' But above all: know when to strike, and when to disappear."

"You listen to me, Adonis. The public doesn't care about who fights better. They care about who commands a room. Parker's unraveling. This is your moment to seize the stage and set fire to everything he thinks he's building. Take the bull by the horns, son. Be the storm, not the cloud."

Adonis nodded slowly, but inside, something was shifting.

Later that afternoon

Caldon returned to Olivia's hidden office, slipping inside with a folder of transcripts, staff interviews, and a USB loaded with security footage.

"He's breaking," Caldon said. "But not the way you think."

Olivia arched an eyebrow. "Explain."

"He's fractured, yes. But his other self doesn't destroy. It protects. It dominates. That's not instability. That's strategy. We let this thing grow too long, and it'll evolve."

Olivia tapped her pen slowly. "And Dave?"

Caldon didn't flinch. "We give him a gentle push off the ledge. Quietly. But we don't make it look like *us*. We make it look like Adonis."

Her eyes flickered. "You're serious?"

Caldon leaned in. "Think about it—Theodore becomes sympathetic. The wounded protector. But if Dave dies and it points to Adonis… you sink two ships with one torpedo."

Olivia's gaze sharpened. "And you'll make the nurse remember it that way?"

"I already started. Her coffee was dosed. She'll recall what I want her to recall—Dave whispering Adonis's name. That's all we'll need."

She leaned back in her chair, almost admiringly. "You're a savage."

Caldon gave her a cool smile. "You didn't hire me for mercy."

What Olivia didn't know was that Caldon had been watching her too. Recording her. Feeding information to her enemies. His end game wasn't loyalty. It was leverage.

Back at City Hall

Theodore's supervisor, Director Brenda Malloy, stood at his desk with a frown. Files stacked up. His chair empty.

"When's the last time Parker showed up?" she asked his coworker.

"Couple days? Maybe more. He left midweek last week looking… off."

Brenda folded her arms. "He's either unraveling or running. Either way, this campaign is interfering with his duties."

She reached for her phone. "Let's schedule a formal wellness evaluation."

CHAPTER EIGHTEEN: THE QUIET BETWEEN THUNDER

Date: August 18, 2004 – 2:13 p.m.

The fluorescent lights of General Duschinni Hospital buzzed overhead as Detective Marcus Cain and his partner, Detective Elena Ruiz, stepped through the main entrance. Both wore their badges clipped to their belts, subtle but commanding.

At the front desk, a young nurse glanced up from her monitor.

"Can I help you?" she asked politely.

"We're here to follow up with Alessia Tolliver regarding the incident with her brother, Dave Tolliver," Marcus said.

Detective Ruiz added, "We're also looking to speak with Theodore Parker. Do you know their whereabouts?"

The nurse bit her lip. "Ms. Tolliver left early. She didn't say where she was going."

Ruiz nodded, about to turn away, but Marcus tilted his head slightly.

"Anything unusual happen since the incident?" he asked.

The nurse hesitated. Her fingers fidgeted with the corner of a clipboard. "Well… someone came by yesterday. Said he was a hospital compliance investigator. He had credentials, but he gave me the creeps."

Marcus raised a brow. "Name?"

"I—I don't remember. He was tall, sharp. Looked like he belonged in a government building. But he asked weird questions. About Theodore Parker."

"What kind of questions?"

"He said Parker wasn't himself during the altercation. Asked if I saw him change. Like, become someone else."

Ruiz exchanged a look with Marcus. He stepped forward.

"Did he leave a card? Anything?"

The nurse shook her head. "But he made me feel like… like I shouldn't trust Mr. Parker. Like he was dangerous."

Marcus narrowed his eyes. "You feel that way now?"

“I—I don’t know. He just made it sound like something was off. He planted the idea.”

Marcus’s gut twisted. Someone was trying to rewrite the narrative.

“Ruiz,” he said quietly, “we need to pull hospital security footage. Find out who this ‘investigator’ really is.”

Date: August 18, 2004 – 9:06 p.m.

Theodore sat in the dim light of Alessia's apartment, shoulders hunched, hands trembling as they clutched a chipped mug of untouched tea. Rain pattered lightly against the windows, casting shifting shadows across the hardwood floor.

Alessia stood near the entryway, arms crossed, jaw tight. Her pain was fresh, visible. Her eyes, once soft and bright, were now guarded.

"I should've protected him," she said bitterly, breaking the silence. "He was spiraling, and I ignored it because I didn’t want to believe what he’d become. And now… now he’s barely clinging to life."

Theodore didn't look up. "It should've been me in that hospital bed. Not Dave."

Alessia's voice cracked. "Don't say that."

"It's true," he whispered. "I lost control. I let Teddy take over and—"

"You saved me," she said sharply. "And you didn't kill him. You stopped when I asked. That matters."

He finally looked at her, eyes glistening. "But what if next time, I don't stop?"

She walked toward him slowly, her steps cautious but purposeful.

"I know about Teddy. I've seen the switch in your eyes. I don't know what he is exactly, but I know you. The real you. And I'm not afraid of him."

He stood up, unsure of what to do with his hands. "You should be."

"No," she said, stepping in closer. "I should be afraid of losing you."

She reached for his hand and guided him gently back to the couch. Then, in one smooth motion, she straddled him, her hands on his shoulders, her breath brushing against his lips.

"You're not a monster, Theo. You're a man who's been torn apart and is still standing. That's who I see."

He stared at her, caught between guilt and longing. "I don't deserve this."

"You deserve love," she whispered.

She leaned in and kissed him. Soft. Sure. The kind of kiss that asks for nothing but gives everything.

Then it deepened. Urgent. Desperate. Their hands moved with hunger, pulling, clutching, shedding the layers that separated them.

They rose in a fevered dance, knocking over a small lamp as Theodore's hand slid beneath her blouse. Alessia tugged at his shirt, nearly tearing it open as they stumbled toward the hallway, lips never parting.

Her laughter broke between gasps as he pressed her against the wall, their bodies pressing together with years of restrained fire. "The door," she managed to say.

He kicked it open. They collapsed onto the bed, clothes falling away like silk in the storm.

Every touch was a revelation. Every kiss a reclamation of something lost.

He kissed down her chest, slowly and reverent, his breath hot against her skin. She arched toward him, nails clawing softly down his back.

She whispered his name. Not out of fear. Out of awe.

He entered her like he belonged there, like he'd always belonged there. And in the rhythm of sweat and tangled limbs, they lost themselves.

Nothing else existed—no elections, no trauma, no fractured psyche. Just the sound of skin against skin, the gasp of breath, the surrender of two broken people finally allowing themselves to feel whole.

Afterward, they lay in a tangle of sheets and silence, their chests rising and falling in rhythm.

Theodore turned his head toward her. "I didn't know I could feel this again."

Alessia, brushing a damp curl from his forehead, smiled faintly. “You just needed someone to remind you.”

And there, in the quiet between thunder, they didn’t need to be perfect.

They only needed to be real.

CHAPTER NINETEEN: WOLVES IN PERFUME

Date: August 20, 2004 – 9:42 a.m.

Earlier that morning, Andrew had bumped into Olivia in the hospital lobby. She was on her phone, dressed in a tailored navy suit, barking orders into her headset. He almost walked past her—almost.

But something made him stop.

"Olivia?" he called gently.

She turned, lowering her sunglasses. "Andrew," she said, her voice equal parts surprise and curiosity. "Didn't expect to see you here."

"I was dropping off some files for the ER chief. But seeing you might've made the trip worth it."

She smirked. "Is that so?"

He took a breath and went for it. "Would you want to grab brunch sometime? Maybe today? I promise not to wear a uniform."

She tilted her head, amused and intrigued. "One drink. One hour."

He grinned. “Deal.”

Date: August 20, 2004 – 11:17 a.m.

Andrew adjusted the collar of his polo shirt as he stood in front of the sleek glass-fronted café near the city square. He wasn't nervous often, but something about Olivia Schumacher brought a certain friction to his usually smooth edges. He caught sight of her before she even arrived—the subtle shift in energy on the sidewalk, the stares she drew from passing strangers.

Olivia arrived dressed to turn heads, and she did. A crisp white dress hugged her like it had been tailored by the gods, her heels clicking like punctuation marks against the pavement. Sunglasses perched on her nose like royalty on a throne.

"You're early," she said, brushing past him with a deliberate flick of her hips to a table by the patio railing.

"You're stunning," he replied, grinning as he pulled her chair out. "Seriously, people are burning their brunch just trying to figure out who you are."

She removed her glasses with flair, eyes glinting. "And here I thought paramedics were only good at chest compressions."

He laughed. "Well, I'm certified in mouth-to-mouth, too. Just saying'."

Olivia chuckled, biting her lip. "Bold. I like bold."

They sat. The mimosas arrived almost immediately, as if pre-ordered. Cameras across the street clicked softly behind parked vehicles.

Andrew lifted his glass. "To being off duty."

"To living dangerously," Olivia said, her smile as sharp as a blade.

They laughed, leaned in, exchanged stories. To anyone watching—and there were *many* watching—they looked like two people caught in a spontaneous, magnetic connection.

But for Olivia, this was a weapon.

Behind the scenes, her assistant texted the photographer: *"Go wide. Make it romantic. Get the smile."*

Date: August 20, 2004 – 12:03 p.m.

Theodore sat in a sterile, beige city office at the Housing and Economic Development Office, his back straight, fingers clenched. Across from him, Director Brenda Malloy reviewed notes while two HR reps looked on silently.

"This isn't disciplinary, Mr. Parker," Malloy said, crossing her legs and leaning forward. "It's a welfare check-in. You've missed several workdays, and the last three reports were turned in late. I need to know you're fit to continue at your post."

Theodore nodded slowly. "I understand. It's just been a… a difficult couple of weeks."

Malloy eyed him carefully. "Look, you're smart, Parker. One of the sharpest analysts I've had on this team. But despite these disappearances, this sudden campaign involvement—it doesn't look good. You don't want to burn credibility on both ends."

He opened his mouth to respond, but his phone buzzed on the desk.

"Should I...?" he asked.

Malloy gestured to it. "If it's urgent."

He picked it up and saw the text from Marcus.

Marcus: *"Check the City View blog. Now."*

With trembling fingers, Theodore opened the browser.

A high-res photo filled the screen: Andrew and Olivia. Laughing. Toes nearly touching. Mimosas raised. Her hand on his forearm.

The headline hit like a hammer: **"Opposite Ends, Unexpected Sparks? Olivia Schumacher and Paramedic Andrew Seen Getting Cozy."**

His stomach dropped. Heat crept into his chest. Betrayal bloomed in a sharp, cold wave.

Malloy noticed his change in posture. "Mr. Parker?"

He didn't respond.

"Is everything okay?"

He stood slowly, his voice barely audible. "I need some air."

Date: August 20, 2004 – 1:40 p.m.

Back in the studio, Olivia sat under the warm lights, her poise immaculate. Charlotte Parker sat across from her, smoking an unlit cigarette for comfort, her mascara slightly smudged.

The red light blinked on. They were live.

"Charlotte," Olivia began, voice honeyed, "Thank you for being here. You've raised a son running for mayor. Quite the journey."

Charlotte smiled too wide. "He always wanted to be something more. Even when he was a stuttering mess, always afraid of his own shadow."

Olivia leaned in. "What was Theodore like as a child?"

Charlotte's laugh was sour. "He was soft. Always crying. Always hiding. I did what I had to do to toughen him up. And now look at him. Pretending to be someone he's not. Acting like some polished leader. I never got the spotlight. But he—he gets applause for speeches I know he rehearses in the mirror to keep his tongue from tripping."

"You sound like you resented that."

"Resent? No. I'm just saying, it’s funny how people only see what you let them. He used to beg me not to send him to school. Said the world was too loud for him. Now he’s trying to run a city?"

Olivia pressed further. "What kind of mother were you during those years?"

Charlotte’s expression tightened. "I did what I had to do. We didn’t have help. His father—gone. Bills piled up. I had dreams too, you know. But they disappeared when he came along."

"Did you love him?"

Charlotte blinked. The silence was thick. "He was mine. I raised him. That counts for something."

"There are rumors he was hospitalized as a child. Mental health issues. Anything you care to share?"

Charlotte leaned in. "There was an incident. He had what they called 'episodes' growing up. Sometimes he’d black out. Get quiet. Or... too quiet. He’d stare right through you."

Olivia's brow lifted. "How far back did that behavior go?"

"Birth, maybe. I had complications during labor. They said it was 'botched'—but they never told me what really went wrong. I woke up in a fog, and everything had changed."

"And his father? We've never heard much about him."

Charlotte paused, fiddling with her cigarette. "I don't remember."

"You don't remember the man you had a child with?"

Charlotte shifted. Her voice wavered. "I... signed an NDA."

The studio went quiet.

Olivia's eyes flared with curiosity. "An NDA? Who would make you sign something like that?"

Charlotte hesitated. "I can't say."

Olivia paused, then smiled faintly. "Let me ask you this: do you think Theodore has a real shot at becoming mayor?"

Charlotte snorted, waving her hand dismissively. "Please. He can't even hold a job for more than a year without spiraling. These people out there cheering for him—they don't know the real Theo. He's good at putting on a show. But leadership? No. He folds under pressure. Always has."

Her tone turned bitter. "It's funny watching everyone fall all over themselves for him now. Like he's some golden boy. No one ever clapped for me when I was struggling to raise him on food stamps and bruised knuckles. Now he gets banners and rallies?"

Olivia tilted her head. "So, you'd say you weren't proud of him?"

Charlotte lit the unlit cigarette with a flick of her lighter, inhaled out of habit, and exhaled dry air. "I'm proud I survived him. That's more than most would say. And when this campaign eats him alive, don't say I didn't warn anyone. He was never built for the top. Too much shadow clinging to him, too many cracks in his foundation."

Olivia leaned back slowly, her mind already moving. Her voice dropped an octave.

"Then I think I have more digging to do."

CHAPTER TWENTY: REACTIONS & RUCKUS

Date: August 20, 2004

It only took twenty minutes.

Twenty minutes from the moment the brunch photos of Olivia Schumacher and Andrew hit the internet to when the story spread like wildfire through phones, inboxes, campaign threads, and city hall breakrooms.

The headline: **"Opposite Ends, Unexpected Sparks?"**

The image: Olivia, radiant and calculating, and Andrew, all smiles and dimples—caught in a moment that looked too romantic to be accidental.

But for those who knew better, who knew *everyone* involved? The reaction was immediate, messy, and downright silly.

Theodore sat in his car outside the City Hall building, gripping the steering wheel like it owed him rent money. He zoomed in on the photo again—Olivia laughing with Andrew like they were auditioning for a toothpaste commercial.

“Was that... was that a toast? With mimosas?” he growled.

He threw his head back dramatically and groaned like a Shakespearean villain betrayed by his best friend. “Et tu, Brute?! With brunch, no less?!”

A pigeon landed on his hood and stared at him. “What?! You too now?”

He rolled up the window and whispered to himself, “This is why I don’t go outside. Love triangles are real and they come with hashtags.”

Alessia was mid-sip of her antioxidant smoothie when her assistant sprinted into the office like someone yelled “fire.”

“Emergency,” the assistant gasped. “Level 5 betrayal.”

Alessia checked the phone, saw the photo, and launched a perfect mist of green smoothie across her desk, hitting a framed motivational quote square in the center: *“Stay calm. Stay focused.”*

“Oh, I’m *focused* alright.”

She stood up, pulled her hair into a bun like she was preparing for psychological combat, and said, “Get me my flats, my coat, and a legally sound excuse to scream in a hospital hallway."

Marcus was in the middle of brushing his teeth, humming off-key, when his phone buzzed with a message titled: *"BRO. Check this."*

He tapped it. Spit. Froze.

Then launched the toothbrush with Olympic precision across the bathroom.

"Oh, that's it. I'm bringing back the taser."

He stared into the mirror, foamy-lipped, and muttered, "This man took CPR class with me and *still* went out with the opposition. Traitor."

Adonis was mid-rep at the gym, flexing in the mirror because of course he was. His campaign manager tossed him a tablet like a grenade.

"What now?" Adonis muttered.

He looked. Blinked. Snorted.

"No way... he actually fell for the Scorpio Trap."

He dropped the dumbbell on his own foot, danced in place like a tap-dancing rhino, then pointed at the ceiling and yelled, "I KNEW she had it in her! That's a chess move in a boxing ring!"

Caldon sat alone in a dim, high-tech surveillance room like a Bond villain on his lunch break. Olivia's brunch photo was up on four different screens.

He stirred his coffee. "Wasn't on the schedule. Impressive."

He tapped through feeds, zoomed in on Andrew's smitten face.

"Poor kid. Walked straight into the Venus flytrap."

He glanced at the room's only security guard, who was busy trying to not laugh.

Caldon smirked. "Cue dramatic music. The credits are about to roll on somebody's feelings."

After a deep sigh, Theodore gathered what was left of his pride and headed back inside City Hall. His face still burned with the sting of betrayal, but his jaw was set—determined.

Director Malloy sat at the same table, sipping lukewarm coffee and flipping through HR documents.

"Welcome back, Mr. Parker," she said dryly, not looking up. "Had your existential crisis?"

"Yep," he muttered. "Turns out betrayal pairs well with humidity."

She raised a brow, then slid a single sheet toward him. "Sign this. You're keeping your position, but we're putting you on limited project visibility until further notice. Wellness checks every Friday. If you so much as sneeze emotionally, I'll know."

He scribbled his signature and stood, offering a quick nod.

As he walked down the corridor, Director Malloy watched from her seat, lips pursed and eyes sharp.

She picked up her office phone.

"Yeah, it's me. Keep an eye on Parker. Something about him feels... off."

CHAPTER TWENTY-ONE: A FINAL BREATH

Date: August 21, 2004 – 7:45 a.m.

The sterile hum of the ICU was quieter than usual, as if the walls themselves knew the gravity of what was about to happen. Rain tapped softly against the window, casting gray shadows that made the room feel more like a tomb than a place of healing. The fluorescents above flickered faintly, bathing everything in a muted glow that felt more funeral than at the hospital.

Dave Tolliver lay still, surrounded by a jungle of tubes and wires. His chest rose and fell with shallow, mechanical effort. A life extended by machines, not by hope.

Alessia sat at his bedside, her fingers wrapped around his limp hand. Her face was calm, but her eyes were glassy—haunted. Her brother. Her baby brother.

And yet, the memory of Maribel's smile—her laugh, her voice—kept slicing through the moment like a knife. He had murdered her best friend. A secret she had only just started to unravel, and one she hadn't spoken aloud. Not yet.

“I don’t know how to mourn you,” Alessia whispered. “I don’t even know if I should.”

Her father, Matthew Tolliver, stood rigid near the foot of the bed. His face was pale and lined with grief that seemed to stretch deeper than sorrow—it was failure. A father who couldn't save his son from himself. A man who had tried to keep the monsters out but never realized they were already inside the house.

“I was supposed to protect you,” he muttered, voice breaking. “I should’ve done more. I should’ve seen it.”

Jessica Tolliver stood behind him, her sobs muffled by a crumpled tissue. “He was just a boy… my boy. No matter what he did, he was ours.”

A nurse stepped into the doorway and nodded solemnly. "It’s time. The attending will be in shortly to begin the process."

Alessia nodded faintly, unable to speak. Her throat tightened.

She leaned in, resting her forehead gently against Dave’s.

"I'm sorry," she breathed. "For everything. For not knowing who you were becoming. For not saving you. For not stopping you."

She pulled back and looked at her father. "This wasn't just addiction. Someone pulled him into this. Used him."

Matthew didn't argue. He just nodded slowly, his jaw clenched to hold back the scream he wouldn't let out.

The machines were silenced one by one.

The final breath passed.

Silent.

Soft.

Gone.

Jessica collapsed into Matthew's arms. Alessia's knees buckled, and she dropped into the chair beside the bed like the weight of her own heart had finally crushed her.

She closed his eyes, kissed his forehead, and whispered, "Rest now, little brother."

But inside her, peace did not bloom.

Only fury.

Elsewhere...

Adonis stood by his office window, sipping whiskey as the morning fog slowly lifted from the coastline. His expression was unreadable.

His aide entered with a single nod. "They pulled life support. He's gone."

Adonis gave a long, cold exhale. "Good. Loose ends only tangle the ambitious."

But behind his eyes, something flickered—calculated, unreadable. And perhaps… unfinished.

Adonis turned from the window, his voice smooth but distant. "Send flowers to the Tolliver family. Something elegant. White lilies and eucalyptus. Include a note that says: *'With deepest sympathy and respect—Adonis Perry.'*"

His aide blinked. "To Alessia as well?"

He nodded. "Yes. Deliver them separately."

The aide gave a slight bow of the head and exited, phone already in hand.

Adonis returned to his desk just as his cell buzzed. Caldon's name flashed on the screen.

He answered without hesitation. "Talk to me."

Caldon's voice was cool as always. "You asked for a meeting. I've cleared my schedule. Today. My place. Two hours."

Adonis narrowed his eyes at the glass. "Good. I've got questions. And I don't like waiting for answers."

Caldon chuckled. "Then don't be late."

The line went dead.

CHAPTER TWENTY-TWO: OF GRAVES AND VOWS

Date: August 22, 2004 – Morning

The gray skies lingered over Duschinni Beach Cemetery like a curtain unwilling to rise. Rain fell lightly, not in a dramatic downpour, but as a steady drizzle—enough to chill the skin and weigh down spirits. The grass was soft and damp beneath heavy shoes, and the scent of wet earth mixed with wilted flowers clung to the morning air.

Dave Tolliver's funeral was subdued, heavy with tension and conflicted grief. The attendees sat in tight, uncomfortable silence beneath rows of black umbrellas. The minister's voice was distant, the words barely cutting through the thick air of judgment, remorse, and guilt.

Alessia stood beside the casket, dressed in a simple black dress, her eyes sunken but dry. She had no tears left to give. Only questions. And a boiling storm in her chest.

Why didn't I see the signs?

Why didn't he come to me?

How did it get this far?

Was he a monster... or was he made into one?

Her fingers were clenched tightly in front of her. She didn't notice how cold they were. She didn't notice the wind. Only the casket. Only Dave.

Matthew Tolliver looked like a statue carved out of regret. His jaw locked. Eyes glassy. He hadn't spoken much since the machines were unplugged. Today, he looked like a man who had aged twenty years overnight.

Jessica Tolliver leaned on him, sobbing softly, her mascara long since surrendered to the rain. She whispered his name repeatedly, like it would bring him back.

Across the aisle stood Marcus Cain, wearing his formal dress blues, his hat tucked beneath his arm. His expression was unreadable, but his eyes scanned the crowd with the quiet caution of a detective at a crime scene. Beside him, Andrew shifted uncomfortably, torn between offering Alessia a hand and respecting her isolation.

Theodore stood at a distance, under a separate umbrella. His face was drawn, pale, and contemplative. He looked not just at the casket, but at Alessia, the Tolliver parents, the mourners—all like puzzle pieces he couldn't yet fit together. His lips moved slightly, as if reciting a prayer or apology.

And then there was Olivia Schumacher. She wore black lace gloves and a feathered hat, and though her eyes were dry, her mouth was a line of solemn dignity. Her presence was quiet—too quiet, like a predator respectful only for the sake of theater.

Alessia's thoughts circled.

What do they know?

What are they hiding?

Why does everything feel... orchestrated?

As the final words were spoken and the casket was lowered, Alessia looked at her brother's name etched into the metal.

David Tolliver – Beloved Son, Cherished Brother.

But Alessia's heart whispered the truth no one dared to speak aloud:

He was also a killer. And he was killed by something far bigger than drugs or madness.

She looked up at the gray clouds and knew—this was not closure.

This was the beginning.

Date: August 22, 2004 – Evening

Julian Perry's wedding was the opposite of the morning's grief: grandiose, excessive, and unapologetically opulent. The venue—a glass-enclosed cliffside estate overlooking the ocean—was draped in cascading white roses and strings of golden lights. Guests were dressed to kill in more ways than one.

The seating arrangement, however, had been curated by chaos.

Alessia Tolliver and Olivia Schumacher sat at the same table, across from one another.

Theodore was placed between Adonis Perry and Caldon—flanked by silence and tension like a political minefield.

Andrew was awkwardly seated beside Michelle Winslow's flirtatious cousin, who mistook his nervousness for charm.

Marcus Cain was placed with members of Julian Perry's inner circle—businessmen and former campaign managers, most of whom stared at him like he'd walked in carrying a warrant.

Even the officiant looked nervous.

Wine flowed faster than the small talk, and beneath every toast was an undertone of ulterior motives.

Alessia barely touched her plate. Her thoughts were with her parents, still recovering from yesterday's heartbreak. Olivia's voice was syrup sweet as she toasted the bride, but her eyes never left Alessia's.

Adonis, the ever-grinning son of the groom, worked the room like a candidate—but occasionally glanced toward Theodore, who was watching everything too closely.

Caldon, dressed immaculately, never left his seat. He simply observed. Like a man already three steps ahead.

The tension was nearing its breaking point.

And the night wasn't over yet.

CHAPTER TWENTY-THREE: BENEATH THE VOWS

Date: August 22, 2004 – Evening Continued

The air inside the reception hall was heavy perfumed with roses, sweat, and unspoken tension. Beneath the gold chandeliers and the shimmer of white silk, something hung in the atmosphere that had nothing to do with love. It was thick, almost visible—suspicion and secrets clinking like ice in champagne glasses.

The toast began.

Michelle's cousin, halfway through her fourth glass of wine, stood and clinked her glass. Her voice rang with tipsy cheer, the volume just a notch too high.

"To Michelle, who finally found a man with money *and* good teeth. And to Julian, who figured out that younger love doesn't always mean yoga instructors and lawsuits!"

Laughter rippled—uneven and strained. Michelle's smile was polite. Julian's face twitched with the urge to roll his eyes.

Adonis rose next, straightening his silk tie, a flawless smirk on his face.

“To my father,” he began. “A man who proves ambition never really ages—it just upgrades its wardrobe. May this union be filled with more passion than prenups, and may Michelle never find his burner phone.”

This time, the laughter was louder—shocked, a little drunk, and mixed with a few gasps. Michelle gripped her wine glass tighter, the smile on her face like porcelain.

Then Olivia stood, tall and poised in midnight-black silk. Her glass sparkled in the light, but her eyes were locked on Alessia.

“To new beginnings,” Olivia said smoothly. “To partnerships built not only on love, but on resilience. May this marriage outlast secrets... and outlive regrets.”

She raised her glass slowly. “And to those who came bearing pain—thank you for still showing up. It takes courage to sit across from the past.”

Alessia didn’t blink. Didn’t flinch. But her nails dug into her palm beneath the tablecloth.

Shady Side Conversations

Caldon leaned into Adonis, their voices hushed near the open bar.

"You asked for truth," Caldon said. "She's circling. Not just Olivia—Alessia. And now Theodore's sniffing around like a bloodhound with trust issues."

Adonis sipped his drink slowly, eyes scanning the ballroom. "Let him sniff. The scents already tainted."

Caldon leaned in further. "Maribel's death... Dave's overdose... It's unraveling faster than expected. We can't hold the leash on this for much longer."

"And Olivia?" Adonis asked.

"She's running her own play," Caldon replied. "If she flips, we burn. She's the only one who knows how deep the well goes."

Adonis narrowed his eyes. "Then make sure she never climbs out of it."

Behind the Kitchen Doors, Marcus cornered Andrew.

"You trust Olivia?" he asked bluntly.

Andrew gave a small shrug. "I don't *not* trust her. She's smart. She challenges me. She's not like anyone I've ever met."

Marcus scoffed. "Yeah, that's usually what they say about volcanoes too—until you're ankle-deep in lava."

Andrew folded his arms. "You think she's dangerous?"

"I think she's playing every angle. And I think you're standing in her blind spot. That makes you disposable."

Andrew looked away for a second, conflicted. "She's not cold. Not with me."

"Yeah? And how many other guys do you think she's fed lines to?" Marcus countered. "You're good with trauma. Use it. Think. Don't get caught with your heart where your instincts should be."

Andrew didn't reply. But his silence spoke volumes.

Near the entryway, Theodore found Alessia standing alone by a floral arrangement, staring out toward the ocean.

"You okay?" he asked gently.

"No," she answered. "You?"

He shook his head. “Not even close.”

They exchanged a look—one filled with fear, grief, and the flicker of something unresolved.

“This place feels like a trap,” Alessia murmured. “Everyone’s smiling like they’re hiding blades.”

Theodore exhaled. “Maybe they are.”

The Stare Downs

Across the ballroom, Olivia and Alessia’s eyes locked again. It was silent warfare—two women carrying history, loss, and secrets in their stares. Olivia’s expression was unreadable, a mask of sophistication. Alessia’s was raw, torn between grief and fury.

Theodore and Adonis caught each other’s glance mid-toast. There was no smirk this time. No nod. Just heat. Theodore’s jaw tightened. Adonis’s eyes gleamed with a challenge.

One of us doesn’t walk out of this clean, Theodore thought.

Caldon? He didn’t stare. He *monitored*. Calm, calculated, ready.

He watched the lies fold in on themselves like dominoes prepped for collapse.

The music picked up. The dance floor buzzed. The night, from the outside, looked perfect. But under the vows and vintage wine, something was festering. Breathing. Waiting.

CHAPTER TWENTY-FOUR: THE BULLET AND THE VOW

Date: August 22, 2004 – 10:37 p.m.

The ballroom shimmered under chandeliers like a masquerade of danger dressed in designer gowns. The music didn't just pick up—it swelled, each beat syncing with the pulse of something invisible building beneath the surface. Laughter turned to forced chuckles. Eyes darted. Smiles grew brittle.

Adonis slipped through the crowd like a man owning the room. His champagne glass full, his charm at maximum voltage. He approached Alessia with a lazy grin and a slow tilt of his head.

"Didn't think you'd come," he said, brushing a stray curl from her shoulder without asking.

Alessia leaned back, just enough for him to notice.

"Didn't think I'd see you smiling," she replied. "Given the week."

Adonis's smile faltered for half a second. "Life goes on, doesn't it?"

Before she could answer, his tone dropped.

"You know... we had something once. Maybe it deserves a second act."

Alessia's eyes narrowed. "Maybe it never had a first act. Just a spotlight on you."

Adonis chuckled, brushing off the burn. "You always did know how to sting, even when you smiled."

She stepped past him toward the dance floor—where Theodore had been watching from the sidelines, tension clinging to him like static.

She moved toward him.

And Adonis saw it.

Something shifted in his expression—confusion? Wounded pride? Or something darker?

Theodore met her halfway. Their hands brushed.

And then—

Pop.

Not the champagne.

A gunshot.

The sound cracked through the room like lightning against velvet.

For a heartbeat, everything paused. Glasses froze midair. Conversations hung unfinished. Then the screams erupted.

Tables toppled. Glass shattered. Silverware clanged to the floor. The orchestra screeched to a halt.

"Down! Everybody down!" someone yelled.

Michelle shrieked. Julian stumbled, pulled back by his security team. Chairs scattered like bones.

The lights flickered.

Marcus dove toward the crowd, drawing his weapon. "Shooter! Where's the goddamn shooter?!"

Alessia fell to her knees, eyes wild. "Theo!"

Theodore turned in a full circle, chest heaving. Smoke or steam hung in the air.

And then—he saw the blood.

A crimson trail leading from the crowd to the edge of the dance floor.

Someone was down.

Someone was groaning.

He ran.

"Move! Move!" he barked, shoving through stunned guests.

And there he was—Andrew—curled on his side, gasping, a red stain spreading fast across his jacket.

"No..." Theodore whispered.

He dropped to his knees. "Andrew. Stay with me. Look at me."

Alessia screamed behind him. "Oh my God. Oh my God!"

Andrew blinked slowly. "Didn't... didn't see it coming."

Theodore grabbed his shoulders. "Who?! Who fired?!"

Andrew coughed blood. "Wasn't... supposed to be me."

His head lolled.

Theodore shouted, “Medic! I need a medic!”

Behind the Curtains

A side door swung shut.

Metal clinked softly—a rifle disassembled with methodical precision.

The silver watch on the gloved wrist—cracked face, smudged glass—was unmistakable.

Caldon exhaled. “Missed. Wrong timing.”

He dropped the gloves in a bin. Checked his burner. A message flashed:

"Abort. Situation evolving."

He vanished down the service hallway without a sound.

Back in the Ballroom

EMTs burst through the doors, cutting a path through the chaos.

Alessia clutched Andrew’s hand, tears streaming down her face. “Don’t you dare leave me,” she whispered.

Marcus shoved through with bloody knuckles and fury in his eyes. “Lock the building. Now. Nobody in or out. I want every exit covered.”

Theodore sat still beside Andrew, blood staining his tuxedo, face numb.

“They were aiming for me,” he said hoarsely.

Marcus crouched beside him. “That’s not paranoia. That’s the truth.”

Then his eyes caught movement—someone in the shadows, near the column.

Charlotte Parker.

Her eyes locked with Theodore’s.

No emotion. No fear.

Only knowing.

The music had stopped.

But the silence screamed louder.

CHAPTER TWENTY-FIVE: SHADOWS AND SHATTERED GLASS

Date: August 23, 2004 – Early Morning

The hospital corridor smelled of antiseptic and too many unanswered questions. Alessia sat alone, her blouse stiff with dried blood, her trembling fingers clutching a Styrofoam cup of untouched coffee. The waiting room clock ticked louder than it should have.

Andrew was in surgery.

She hadn't slept. Couldn't. Her mind replayed the moment over and over—the music, the shot, the chaos, the scream. The way his body folded like a marionette whose strings had been violently severed.

She looked up at the hallway monitor. Still in critical condition.

Marcus stepped in, dark circles under his eyes, blood still on his cuffs. "They pulled security footage from the rooftop. Somebody cut the camera feed two hours before the reception started. Clean. Professional."

Alessia blinked. "You think it was planned?"

"I think someone knew exactly where the exits were. And who the target was." He pulled a small evidence bag from his coat. Inside, a security pass. "Found this near the west service door. Not on the guest list."

She stared at it. Her gut twisted. "It wasn't supposed to be Andrew."

"No. It was Theodore."

Somewhere Else in the City

Caldon watched the morning news silently from a glass-walled apartment downtown. The headline: *"Mayoral Candidate's Campaign Advisor Shot at Wedding Reception."* His reflection smirked back at him in the screen.

He stirred his coffee. Dialed a burner.

"It's in motion," he said. "The fault lines are shifting."

On the other end, Olivia's voice crackled. "I heard. You took the shot?"

"It was clean. Until it wasn't. He moved. Andrew got in the way."

"Damn it, Caldon. You were supposed to wait. There were too many variables."

"There always are. But if we wait, we lose initiative. You told me to act when the asset became unstable. Theodore is unraveling. The photo was leaked. The hospital files are surfacing."

"We weren't ready to handle the fallout. Not yet."

He took a slow sip of his coffee. "We are now. The board's reset. All three candidates are under scrutiny. And Parker? He's going to either break—or become a weapon."

Olivia exhaled. "And Charlotte?"

"She's ready to burn it all down. Especially now that her truth might finally matter."

"I'm not convinced she'll stay in line."

"She doesn't need to stay in line. She just needs to speak at the right time."

There was a long silence between them.

"You're playing both sides again, aren't you?" Olivia asked.

Caldon smiled faintly. "It's the only way to survive when the board collapses."

They stared at the hospital lights in silence.

The storm wasn't coming.

It was already here.

CHAPTER TWENTY-SIX: THREADS IN THE DARK

Date: August 24, 2004 – Morning

Marcus Cain sat in his unmarked cruiser, engine idle, eyes scanning the nondescript brick building across the street. It was a small private security firm that operated like a ghost—minimal website, no front desk, just a buzzer and a reinforced steel door. The fake pass he'd found at the wedding matched a batch produced by this location.

The building felt more like a bunker than an office. He stepped out, adjusted his holster beneath his coat, and crossed the street with the calm of a man who'd walked into gunfire and outlived it.

Inside, the lobby was cold and sterile. No decor. No branding. A single desk occupied the space, behind which sat a lanky man with thinning hair and a hollow smile.

"Detective Cain," Marcus announced, flashing his badge with a sharp flick. "I'm here for ID logs, camera records, and any employee with the initials D.G. in the last week."

The man blinked. "Do you have a warrant?"

Marcus leaned forward, voice low and lethal. "I've got a bleeding campaign advisor, a wedding full of traumatized witnesses, and a pass traced back to this dump. If I have to call for a warrant, I'm dragging this whole building into the media grinder. So unless you want reporters camped on your doorstep asking why your IDs are showing up at shooting scenes, get me the damn logs."

The receptionist paled and stood. "Give me ten minutes."

"Make it five."

He returned with a supervisor, who handed over a tablet.

"These are the most recent logs. That batch was issued on August 20th to a subcontractor. Temporary clearance, no name attached."

Marcus scrolled. "That's not good enough."

He pulled up the badge number from memory. "Run this through your facial recognition logs. And open up your security footage from that day."

More hesitation. Marcus slammed a palm down on the desk. "Now."

The footage flickered to life. A tall figure walked through a back hallway. Ball cap. Collared shirt. But then—he turned. The camera caught a faint profile.

Marcus paused it. Zoomed.

A glint of a cracked silver watch.

"Stop. Go back two seconds."

The image sharpened just enough. Caldon.

He stepped back from the screen, every muscle wired tight.

"What did he access?"

The supervisor clicked through logs. "Looks like he requested a custom batch of guest passes. No names, just blank credentials. Picked them up in person. Paid in cash."

Marcus scribbled in his notebook.

"Did he say anything?"

The receptionist, still rattled, said quietly, "Just one thing when he left. He looked at the door and said, 'Sometimes the easiest way in… is to walk like you belong there.'"

Marcus stared at him, expression unreadable.

"Print every frame. Every log. If this leaks before I say so, I'll be back—with a search warrant and a forensic unit."

He left without another word, heart pounding but face cold.

Outside, the city buzzed, oblivious.

But Marcus knew—someone had declared war, and he intended to return fire.

Elsewhere – City Hall Steps

Adonis Perry adjusted his cufflinks and gave the press a tired but charming smile. But behind his eyes, the storm churned.

"What happened at the wedding is a tragedy," he said into the array of microphones, "but let's not mistake chaos for leadership. This city needs direction, not disorder. It needs vision, not silence. While others disappear behind hospital curtains and excuses, I'm still here. Still standing. Still serving."

His voice rose with fervor.

"Now, more than ever, we need to ask ourselves—do we want a leader who chokes on public pressure and hides behind sympathy? Or do we want a man who can face crisis head-on, not from a stretcher?"

Behind him, a massive banner unfurled:

ADONIS PERRY – ORDER. VISION. PERRY.

He shook hands, smiled for the cameras, but beneath the polish was a man unraveling. His polling numbers were flatlined. Internal metrics showed a 9% drop overnight. Whispers floated like smoke through the corridors of power:

- "Adonis knew the shooter."
- "He's too close to Olivia."
- "What is Julian Perry hiding?"

And worse— "Parker might actually win."

Inside Perry Campaign HQ – Closed-Door Meeting

The room was ice cold from overworked air conditioning, but Adonis was sweating. His jaw was tight. His hand slammed down hard on a polished oak table as he threw a folder toward his staff.

"I want Theodore Parker disqualified. Finished. Eviscerated. I don't care if you have to leak his childhood dental records—get something that scares voters."

His communications director spoke cautiously. "Sir, we've flagged his medical file—there are inconsistencies. Some... potential behavioral indicators, but it's thin."

"Thin?!" Adonis barked. "He's been institutionalized. He has mental breaks. And now, conveniently, he's the public's wounded darling because someone took a shot at him and missed?!"

"We're trying to avoid the appearance of desperation," another aide offered.

Adonis spun on him. "We are desperate. Do you not see what's happening? If this election were today, I'd lose. To *him*. To a man who stutters through interviews and talks like a lost puppy. And now he's suddenly a hero?"

He pounded the table again. "Leak it. All of it. I want headlines that burn. I want the voters to see that Theodore Parker is *unstable*, *unfit*, and *unworthy* of this office."

A long silence filled the room.

The campaign manager nodded slowly. “It’ll be done.”

Adonis exhaled, ran a hand through his hair, and turned to the window.

Below, a protest sign waved in the distance. It read: *“Theodore for Tomorrow.”*

He stared at it for a long time.

And for the first time in weeks—he felt fear.

CHAPTER TWENTY-SEVEN: FIRE AND PROMISE

Date: August 25, 2004 – Early Evening

The crowd outside the downtown convention plaza pulsed like a living thing—thousands deep, waving signs in rhythmic unison:

PARKER FOR PROGRESS, THEODORE FOR TOMORROW, VOICE OF THE PEOPLE.

The energy buzzed like static electricity before a storm.

Theodore stood backstage, flanked by two campaign aides. He adjusted his collar, tried to swallow the tightness in his throat. This was the first public appearance since the wedding shooting. Since Andrew.

"You ready?" his aide asked, checking his earpiece.

"I don't feel ready," Theodore admitted.

"You're not supposed to. You're supposed to walk out there and *be* ready."

He nodded, staring at the curtain that separated him from the city.

The music swelled, and the emcee's voice echoed across the plaza: "Duschinni Beach—please welcome your candidate for change, for heart, for tomorrow—Theodore Parker!"

The curtain drew back. The light hit him hard.

The noise surged.

He stepped to the podium, hands gripping the sides, heart pounding.

He took a breath. And spoke.

"I wasn't supposed to be here tonight," he began. "Hell, I wasn't supposed to be anywhere but a hospital room, praying for my friend to wake up. But the people of this city deserve honesty. And I've never been more certain that we are at a crossroads."

The crowd fell silent.

"We can keep pretending the old guard still cares. That politics as usual still serves the people. Or—we can demand more."

He scanned the crowd. "I've been mocked. I've been doubted. I've been told I'm too quiet, too uncertain, too...

broken." He paused, voice steadying. "But broken things still hold value. And sometimes they hold the truth better than anything else."

A wave of applause rolled over him.

"I'm not perfect. But I know what this city feels like when it forgets you. And I will not forget *you*."

The applause rose into cheers, chants of *PARKER, PARKER* echoing off buildings.

Backstage, one of his aides beamed. But in the crowd, a few figures stood motionless—silent, watching.

Near the stage's edge, a group of hecklers began shouting: "WHERE'S DAVE? WHO'S TEDDY?"

Security shifted. The crowd booed. Theodore paused, staring straight at them.

"No more secrets," he said into the mic, eyes sharp. "We've all lost someone. We all carry ghosts. But I won't be haunted by mine. I'll face them. With you."

The tension broke into thunderous support.

Across Town – Olivia Schumacher's Rally

At a sleek arts venue on the east side, Olivia's rally carried a different energy—elegant, curated, upscale. Supporters wore pins labeled *SCHUMACHER FOR SOLUTIONS* and sipped cocktails as jazz music transitioned into a commanding drumbeat.

Olivia walked onto stage in a crisp cream pantsuit, her hair swept back, her gaze steely.

"Leadership is not a popularity contest," she said. "It's a responsibility. One I've carried longer than most of my opponents have held a job."

Subtle applause rolled through the crowd.

"We cannot be swept up by sympathy or distraction. What this city needs isn't a wounded idealist. It needs a strategist. A tactician. Someone who knows how to navigate broken systems—not just mourn them."

There were quiet murmurs of approval. She leaned in to the mic.

"We can't afford emotion. We need execution."

Her rally ended with a controlled burst of energy—slick video segments, clean lighting, coordinated chants. But beneath it all, there was calculation. Intent.

As she left the stage, she whispered to her campaign manager, "Let Parker have his moment. When the time comes, they'll see what he really is."

Meanwhile – In a Darkened Car Near Theodore's Rally

Caldon watched through binoculars. Next to him, a digital recorder blinked red.

"He's becoming dangerous," he muttered.

Beside him, a phone buzzed with a message: *"Charlotte interview scheduled. September 1st. Evening broadcast."*

He pocketed the phone and started the engine.

"Let the secrets burn."

CHAPTER TWENTY-EIGHT: BEHIND CLOSED DOORS, BENEATH THE SURFACE

Date: August 26, 2004 – Afternoon into Night

Detective Marcus Cain - Blood in the Water

The sky over West Duschinni Beach was the color of gunmetal. Detective Marcus Cain leaned against his unmarked cruiser, his eyes on the front door of a greasy, barely-holding-on diner. Neon flickered and buzzed over the sign — *Tony's Grill*. The kind of place forgotten by time but remembered by cops who liked privacy.

Detective Eugene Greene pulled up slow, killing his engine and stepping out with a grunt. "Marcus Cain," he said, chewing the inside of his cheek, "you don't call me unless it's bad."

Marcus nodded once, grim. "It's worse."

Inside the diner, over black coffee and old scars, Marcus laid it out. Maribel's death wasn't a random act of violence. Someone paid for precision. The name Caldon slithered across the table like venom.

Greene sat back, blowing out a breath. "Shit... Caldon's still breathing? That ghost still doing contract work?"

Marcus's tone was lethal. "Not just breathing. He's pulling strings around Julian Perry's empire. And I got hard evidence — bribes to hospital staff, altered files, fake IDs traced back to Caldon."

Greene cursed under his breath. "You digging this deep, Cain, you better be ready to bury bodies or be buried yourself."

Marcus grinned coldly. "Oh, I'm ready for either."

Alessia Tolliver - Shattered Truth

The hum of the fluorescent lights in the hospital records room was a sharp buzz that drilled into Alessia Tolliver's skull. Her heart was in her throat, pounding.

Twin A — Released to Charlotte Parker. Twin B — Redacted.

Her cursor hovered over the fine print until she caught the line that made her blood run ice-cold:

Transfer Approved By: Julian Perry — Executive Authorization.

Alessia whispered, “Julian Perry... signed off on this?”

Her knees went weak. The pieces fell together like shattered glass rearranging into clarity. Maribel must’ve found this. Maribel must have died for this.

Her eyes shifted to the photo of Maribel on her desk. “You were onto something, Mari... something no one wanted found.”

Charlotte Parker - The Interview from August 20, 2004 – 1:40 PM

Previously recorded interview-Date: August 20, 2004 – 1:40 p.m.

Back in the studio, Olivia sat under the warm lights, her poise immaculate. Charlotte Parker sat across from her, smoking an unlit cigarette for comfort, her mascara slightly smudged.

The red light blinked on. They were live.

"Charlotte," Olivia began, voice honeyed, "Thank you for being here. You’ve raised a son running for mayor. Quite the journey."

Charlotte smiled too wide. "He always wanted to be something more. Even when he was a stuttering mess, always afraid of his own shadow."

Olivia leaned in. "What was Theodore like as a child?"

Charlotte's laugh was sour. "He was soft. Always crying. Always hiding. I did what I had to do to toughen him up. And now look at him. Pretending to be someone he's not. Acting like some polished leader. I never got the spotlight. But he—he gets applause for speeches I know he rehearses in the mirror to keep his tongue from tripping."

"You sound like you resented that."

"Resent? No. I'm just saying, it's funny how people only see what you let them. He used to beg me not to send him to school. Said the world was too loud for him. Now he's trying to run a city?"

Olivia pressed further. "What kind of mother were you during those years?"

Charlotte's expression tightened. "I did what I had to do. We didn't have help. His father—gone. Bills piled up. I had dreams too, you know. But they disappeared when he came along."

"Did you love him?"

Charlotte blinked. The silence was thick. "He was mine. I raised him. That counts for something."

"There are rumors he was hospitalized as a child. Mental health issues. Anything you care to share?"

Charlotte leaned in. "There was an incident. He had what they called 'episodes' growing up. Sometimes he'd black out. Get quiet. Or... too quiet. He'd stare right through you."

Olivia's brow lifted. "How far back did that behavior go?"

"Birth, maybe. I had complications during labor. They said it was 'botched'—but they never told me what really went wrong. I woke up in a fog and everything had changed."

"And his father? We've never heard much about him."

Charlotte paused, fiddling with her cigarette. "I don't remember."

"You don't remember the man you had a child with?"

Charlotte shifted. Her voice wavered. "I... signed an NDA."

The studio went quiet.

Olivia's eyes flared with curiosity. "An NDA? Who would make you sign something like that?"

Charlotte hesitated. "I can't say."

Olivia paused, then smiled faintly. "Let me ask you this: do you think Theodore has a real shot at becoming mayor?"

Charlotte snorted, waving her hand dismissively. "Please. He can't even hold a job for more than a year without spiraling. These people out there cheering for him—they don't know the real Theo. He's good at putting on a show. But leadership? No. He folds under pressure. Always has."

Her tone turned bitter. "It's funny watching everyone fall all over themselves for him now. Like he's some golden boy. No one ever clapped for me when I was struggling to raise him on food stamps and bruised knuckles. Now he gets banners and rallies?"

Olivia tilted her head. "So, you'd say you weren't proud of him?"

Charlotte lit the unlit cigarette with a flick of her lighter, inhaled out of habit, and exhaled dry air. "I'm proud I survived him. That's more than most would say. And when this campaign eats him alive, don't say I didn't warn anyone. He was never built for the top. Too much shadow clinging to him, too many cracks in his foundation."

Olivia leaned back slowly, her mind already moving. Her voice dropped an octave.

"Then I think I have more digging to do."

Caldon - The Puppet Master

Inside a dark, silent bar smelling of whiskey and old regret, Caldon slid a hard drive across the table to a contact shrouded in shadow.

"This is Parker. Everything. Medical. Psychological. His roots."

The contact shifted. "Olivia wants leverage. Not a body count."

Caldon's voice was a gravel-filled promise. "She's getting both."

His phone buzzed. A new message:

"Target is moving. Theodore Parker. Alone. Vulnerable."

Caldon smirked faintly. "Time to close the circle."

Alessia's voice cracked over the line, raw and urgent. "Marcus... meet me tonight. It's about Theodore. It's about *everything*."

Marcus's voice was a low growl of a man walking willingly into war. "Where?"

"General Duschinni Hospital parking garage. Level 3."

Marcus hung up, sliding his badge onto his belt like a soldier strapping on armor.

"This city's about to bleed truth, Alessia. And no one's walking away clean."

CHAPTER TWENTY-NINE: FRACTURES BENEATH THE SURFACE

Date: August 27, 2004 – Early Morning

Andrew In The Hospital

The rhythmic beep of the heart monitor filled the room like a ticking clock inside Andrew's hospital room at General Duschinni Hospital. It was a low, steady reminder of how close life and death were playing with his body.

Theodore sat slumped in a chair near the bed, elbows on his knees, staring blankly at the scuffed tile floor.

"I'm sorry, man..." Theodore whispered to Andrew's unmoving frame. "We were just supposed to have each other's backs. Now you're laid up in here because of me... because I keep dragging everyone I care about into this war."

He laughed bitterly, wiping his hand over his face. "And I don't even know how this ends anymore. But whatever happens... I'll protect Alessia. I swear to you."

Suddenly, a rasped whisper cut through the silence like a knife.

"Protect... her..."

Theodore's head shot up. "Andrew?"

Andrew's lips barely moved, eyelids fluttering against exhaustion and medication. But the message was clear.

Protect Alessia.

Marcus and Alessia - In The Parking Garage

Level 3 echoed with isolation, the concrete floor like a slab of tension beneath their feet.

Alessia handed Marcus the USB drive, her hands trembling slightly.

"This changes everything," she said, voice hollow and worn. "Julian Perry signed off on separating them. Theodore and Adonis... they're connected by blood."

Marcus clenched his jaw hard enough it felt like it might crack.

"Two brothers... raised on lies," Marcus muttered. "Both walking weapons... and they don't even know who loaded them."

Suddenly, both their phones vibrated simultaneously.

Breaking News Alert: *Exclusive Interview — Charlotte Parker Unleashed*

Their eyes met in shared dread.

Reactions Across The City - Charlotte's Interview Airs

Televisions glowed across bars, homes, offices — playing Charlotte Parker's raw, venom-laced interview.

In Theodore's hospital room, he sat frozen, watching his own mother cut him to pieces on live TV.

Charlotte's final words burned through the screen:

"He was never built for the top. Too much shadow clinging to him, too many cracks in his foundation."

Theodore's heart felt like lead in his chest.

Adonis Perry stood in his penthouse, watching with boiling rage.

"This woman is going to burn it all down..."

But beneath the rage was something else.

Fear.

Alessia in the parking garage covered her mouth in shock.

"She's poisoning him... the whole city... turning him into the villain."

Marcus's voice was steel. "Olivia's fingerprints are all over this. Every line Charlotte just spit out... was coached."

But Marcus didn't move. Didn't blink.

Something wasn't right. Something Charlotte said scratched at an old scar in Marcus's memory.

"Marcus? What's wrong?" Alessia asked, her pulse racing.

Marcus's eyes darkened like a storm was building inside his skull.

"That line... 'I don't remember' — about Theodore's father... That's a lie. That's a big, deliberate lie."

His voice dropped even lower.

"Charlotte's got a lot of sins, but forgetting Julian Perry? That ain't one of them."

Slowly, Marcus reached into his coat pocket — pulling out a battered, yellowed field notebook. Notes from a cold case years ago.

Alessia's heart nearly stopped.

Marcus flipped to a page —

Cold Case 1980 — Domestic Disturbance.

Name: *Charlotte Parker — Witness*

In fading ink underneath: *Altercation involving Julian Perry.*

Alessia staggered back, her face drained of all color.

"No... no... Julian Perry?"

Marcus's face was cold stone.

"Charlotte didn't forget Theodore's father... She was told to. She was paid to. Or threatened to. Either way..."

He shut the notebook with finality.

"Theodore's father has been in plain sight all along. Julian Perry."

Silence swallowed them whole.

Alessia whispered in horror, like saying the name summoned darkness itself.

"Dear God... it *was* always him."

Theodore - Alone With His Demons

Outside the hospital, Theodore walked beneath the glow of tired streetlights, haunted by Charlotte's words, haunted by Teddy's voice.

Teddy's voice was stronger now — colder... deadlier.

"They buried the truth, Theo... but blood never stays buried forever. It rises. It screams. And it remembers."

From the darkness... movement.

Caldon.

Watching.

Hunting.

Waiting.

The hunter had arrived.

CHAPTER THIRTY: THE WOLVES SHED THEIR MASKS

Date: August 28, 2004 — 4 Days Before Election Day

Flashback - When The Knife Sank Deep

Late Night — Adonis Perry's Penthouse — August 27, 2004

The lights of Duschinni Beach stretched far beyond the glass windows of Adonis Perry's penthouse, but none of it mattered.

Adonis sat in the darkness, drink untouched, staring at the television — the last of Charlotte Parker's interview replaying in his mind like a siren he couldn't silence.

Then came the soft click of his private elevator.

Caldon.

Always appearing like a shadow where fear lives.

Adonis didn't turn around. His voice was gravel.

"What do you want, Caldon? Come to finish burying me?"

Caldon's voice was silk over steel. "No, Adonis... I came to unearth you."

Adonis finally turned, rage in his eyes. "Cut the riddles. Say what you came here to say."

Caldon stepped closer, holding a thin black file in his gloved hands. The kind of file meant to change lives or destroy them.

He laid it on the table between them.

"Julian Perry has two sons. Not one."

Adonis froze.

Caldon’s stare never wavered. "Born minutes apart. Different worlds. One raised in a kingdom. One left in the gutter."

He tapped the file with deadly precision.

"Theodore Parker... isn’t just your rival. He’s your blood. Your brother."

The silence was suffocating.

Adonis staggered back like he'd been gut-punched by reality itself.

"You're lying..."

Caldon's reply was a whisper that could split bone.

"I don't lie, Adonis. Especially not about blood. Blood tells the truth... even when fathers won't."

Adonis's breath hitched — fury rising to a level beyond anything he'd known.

"He... he left me to fight for scraps while that bastard Parker didn't even know he was royalty?"

Caldon's voice dropped like a hammer.

"Your father didn't raise heirs, Adonis... he bred weapons. And now — you're pointed straight at each other."

Adonis's rage turned quiet — too quiet.

"Then I'll show them both... what happens when they create a weapon and forget who loaded it."

The Father & Son War

Julian's private study felt like a crypt — ancient, heavy with the scent of cigar smoke and old wood. Adonis barged in, uninvited, unhinged.

"You sat back," Adonis growled, "while I broke myself for your approval. And all this time... Parker was your blood."

Julian, seated like a king on a worn leather throne, didn’t even blink. "You were never bred to inherit. You were bred to enforce."

Adonis’s jaw clenched. "Is that what I am to you? A weapon? Disposable?"

Julian’s lip curled. "Exactly. And you’ve grown dull."

Adonis exploded, knocking a decanter of whiskey from the table. Glass shattered like his pride.

Julian rose slowly, cold steel in human form. "Theodore survived hell. You survived comfort. That’s the difference between a man forged in fire and a man who hides behind it."

Julian leaned in, his voice a dagger:

"Challenge me again... and I will bury you beneath this city alongside every mistake I’ve ever made."

Adonis stood still, boiling rage in his bones.

***

Midnight was unforgiving.

Caldon's shadow crew moved with surgical precision, abducting Michelle Winslow-Perry from Julian's estate gardens.

No alarms. No mess. Just fear.

But Caldon didn't stash Michelle just anywhere. He delivered her to one of Olivia Schumacher's private estates — miles from the city — framing her by association.

Left behind for Julian was Michelle's wedding ring and a burner phone.

Text message:

"If the King won't bleed, the Queen will."

***

The Queen's Cold Smile

Upon learning of Michelle's abduction, Olivia's reaction was bone-chilling.

She swirled her wine glass, a slow grin forming.

"Tell Caldon... war it is. But make sure he knows... queens don't fall easily."

Her mind raced — not with fear — but with strategy.

***

Marcus and Alessia sat in the shadows of an unmarked car, the city around them boiling over.

"Michelle's gone," Alessia whispered. "Taken from Julian's fortress."

Marcus's voice was pure gravel:

"This isn't politics anymore. This is blood war. And in war... everybody bleeds."

***

Alone in his apartment, Theodore stared into his mirror — Teddy at his shoulder like a ghost he could no longer ignore.

Teddy's voice was darker now, more real:

"They raised weapons, Theo. But they forgot one thing... we don't need permission to burn them down."

Theodore’s reflection was steady, dangerous:

"Then let’s finish this."

***

Julian sat at his desk, the city's king unmasked at last.

His phone buzzed — a single image:

Michelle. Bound. Terrified. Inside a property Julian knew all too well — Olivia Schumacher’s forgotten estate.

Julian’s jaw tightened, eyes darkening to something primal.

He spoke to his bodyguard:

"Prepare the car. Assemble my war council."

Under his breath, with absolute finality:

"They’ve forgotten who rules this city. Time to remind them."

CHAPTER THIRTY-ONE: BLOOD NEVER LIES

Date: August 29, 2004 — 3 Days Before Election Day

Night blanketed Duschinni Beach like a funeral shroud. Julian Perry's convoy rolled through the city streets like a blackened artery pulsing with war.

Inside the lead SUV, Julian sat calm. Inhuman. Ice over rage.

"Breach her estate. Retrieve my wife. Eliminate anyone standing. Leave no questions. No survivors."

At Olivia Schumacher's estate, the tension could slice bone.

Her security teams moved like shadows in perfect sync.

"Positions," she commanded, barefoot, calm, sipping tea by candlelight like the apocalypse meant nothing.

"Let them come. Kings have armies. Queens have castles."

Julian's men breached the estate.

Silenced shots barked death.

Olivia's elite fired back with surgical precision. Every bullet ripping through silk-draped halls. Blood sprayed on priceless art. Death felt personal.

Bodies folded like cards.

Slow-motion carnage.

The smell of gunpowder thick like iron and blood.

The estate roared with agony.

At last, Julian reached Olivia.

Smoke curling around them like old sins.

Olivia stood alone, bleeding from a graze to her temple. Defiant. Regal. Cursed.

"Where's Michelle?" Julian demanded.

Olivia stared cold.

"I don't have her. I never did."

Julian froze.

His mind, calculating, deadly, realized the unforgivable.

"Then who does?"

Beep. Beep. Beep.

Julian turned.

Underneath the war table... a blinking device.

No time to scream.

BOOM.

***

Olivia was dragged from the rubble by her last remaining guard.

Her world burned behind her.

Sirens howled.

In the ER at Duschinni Beach General Hospital, she watched through swollen eyes as news anchors savaged her name. Offshore accounts frozen. Properties seized. Allies gone.

She lay broken but alive.

Then she saw it.

A single white card placed on her nightstand.

Michelle's handwriting.

"Checkmate."

Olivia closed her eyes, a single tear slicing down her ash-stained cheek.

Far from the carnage, Michelle toasted Caldon in their luxury suite.

City lights gleamed beneath them like prey.

"Blood never lies, Caldon," Michelle purred. "But it makes the most beautiful stains."

***

Marcus pieced together intercepted communications.

"She staged it all..."

Alessia's voice was hollow.

"Michelle orchestrated this whole war... from the shadows."

Theodore watched the city burn on TV.

Teddy stood beside him in the mirror, clear as a brother forged in trauma.

"The kings are bleeding, Theo... the queens are dying."

Theodore smiled darkly.

"Sounds like our time."

A package waited at Theodore's door.

Inside:

Michelle's wedding ring.

And a note:

"Your move, Parker."

CHAPTER THIRTY-TWO: WHEN WOLVES HUNT WOLVES

Date: August 30, 2004 — 2 Days Before Election Day

Night gripped Duschinni Beach in silence. Caldon moved like death incarnate — gloves tightened, silencer screwed into place, his steps precise, ghostly.

Tonight, the Parker boy dies.

His eyes scanned Theodore's apartment from across the street, blending into the shadows like the seasoned predator he was.

Miles away in her glass fortress, Michelle watched Caldon through security feeds like a deity of chaos.

She sipped dark red wine, smiling faintly.

"Time to clean house."

An encrypted message slid to Marcus Cain's private line:

"Outside Parker's residence. Ghost needs burying."

Marcus' unmarked cruiser sliced through traffic, sirens dark, lights off.

Alessia sat beside him, pulse racing.

"If anything happens to Theo—"

Marcus cut her off, cold and focused.

"Nothing's happening to Parker tonight but breathing. Caldon's done."

Marcus confronted Caldon outside Theodore's building — gun drawn, voice commanding like a lion.

A small Duschinni Beach PD taskforce fanned out behind Marcus — tactical vests, rifles ready.

But for Marcus? This wasn't just police work. This was personal.

"Marcus Cain, Duschinni Beach Police Department. You're under arrest for conspiracy, attempted murder, unlawful surveillance, and enough criminal acts to lock you under the prison."

Caldon turned, slow grin forming.

"Cute speech."

Gunfire exploded. Tactical precision.

Marcus shot Caldon in the leg, dropped him hard, cuffing him without hesitation.

"Rights are the least of your problems, ghost. You're done haunting this city."

Alessia stormed up to Theodore's apartment, raw emotion burning behind her eyes.

She burst through the door.

Theodore stood in the shadows — eyes dark, body tense.

Without words, Alessia crashed into him, their lips crashing, their hands pulling at each other like starved lovers.

He lifted her, carried her to the bed, laid her down, and drove into her with a powerful missionary rhythm — primal, desperate.

Alessia clawed at the sheets, her knuckles whitening as the pressure inside her built to unbearable heights.

Her voice broke in a loud, shattered scream of surrender:

"THEODORE! Ohhh God—THEODORE!"

Her body arched, shaking violently beneath him as the most intense orgasm of her life ripped through her body, leaving her breathless, glowing, utterly his.

***

Adonis kicked in the penthouse door — expecting Julian.

Instead?

Michelle sat in a sleek, black dress like sin carved in flesh, legs crossed, drink in hand.

She smiled like a serpent.

"Looking for Daddy? Tsk tsk... wrong predator."

Adonis's face twisted in fury.

Michelle purred, voice dipped in seductive poison.

"Come now, Adonis... let's talk legacy. Yours. Mine. And the brother you can't outrun... no matter how hard you try."

Her eyes glinted like knives.

"Sit down, baby wolf... class is in session."

CHAPTER THIRTY-THREE: THE QUEEN'S HEIR

Date: August 31, 2004 — 1 Day Before Election Day

The silence in the penthouse was eerie.

Michelle's eyes stayed locked on Adonis, who stood in the doorway, chest still heaving, sweat dampening his collar. His hands were clenched, veins bulging, teeth grinding beneath his jaw. The fury from chasing ghosts, hunting his father, and finding only her—it still roared inside him.

She didn't flinch. Instead, she poured two glasses of deep amber bourbon and held one out to him like an offering to a restless god.

"You're burning," she whispered. "Let it cool."

Adonis didn't take the glass immediately. He stared at her—at the low-cut black dress clinging to her curves, at the knowing glint in her eye, at the calm power in her posture.

Finally, he took the glass, downing half in a single swallow.

Michelle took a delicate sip from hers, watching the anger in him soften by degrees. The drug in the bourbon was subtle. It wouldn't make him collapse, just drift... lower his defenses... slow his pulse.

She moved toward him, step by step, hips swaying with intent.

"You wanted to find Julian. But he’s not the king anymore. You are."

Adonis blinked, the room a little too warm now. His skin tingled. His muscles relaxed.

She was in front of him now, her fingers grazing his shirt buttons.

"He built power through fear. But I see something deeper in you. Hunger. Will. Fire."

She kissed him. Soft at first. Then deeper.

His resistance weakened. He dropped the empty glass.

She took his hands, guided him to the couch. Straddled him. Pressed her mouth to his neck.

"I don't want your loyalty," she whispered against his ear. "I want your heir."

He groaned, half in confusion, half in desire, as she reached between them and guided his erection inside her.

She rode him with a slow, sensual rhythm that pulsed with purpose.

"With you... I'll create a dynasty. With you, I'll erase him."

Her eyes blazed down into his, controlling every inch of him, every beat of his weakening heart.

He gripped her hips, gasping, head tilting back.

But she owned the tempo.

And the purpose.

When she came, she bit down on his shoulder, marking him.

"My king," she whispered.

He collapsed back into the cushions, dizzy, dazed.

She rose slowly, fixing her dress without shame.

Then she walked to a panel in the wall, pressed her palm, and revealed a hidden screen—showing Julian.

Bound. Gagged. Bloodied.

Michelle watched the feed, her smile widening.

"Don’t worry, darling," she purred. "Your replacement is already inside me."

She turned to Adonis one last time.

"Rest now, baby wolf. Your future just began."

CHAPTER THIRTY-FOUR: SCARRED STRATEGIES

Date: August 31, 2004 — 1 Day Before Election Day

The Quiet Visitor

The fluorescent lights in the hospital cast long shadows across Olivia Schumacher's recovery room. She lay in silence, bandaged, bruised, watching her empire crumble through muted news coverage.

Her skin still burned from the explosion, but it was the silence—no assistants, no backers, no empire—that hurt worse.

The door opened without a knock.

Andrew stepped inside, limping slightly, arm still bandaged, but upright. Alive. More human than anyone she'd seen in days.

Her eyes narrowed. "Come to gloat?"

Andrew pulled up a chair and sat.

"No. I came to look you in the eyes… and see if there's anything left worth saving."

Olivia laughed, bitter and brittle. “Save me? Don’t flatter yourself, paramedic.”

“I saved lives in that explosion,” he said calmly. “While your empire tried to kill ‘em.”

She looked away.

“I saw you on that stage,” Andrew said, voice even. “Powerful. Controlled. Cold. And now?” He gestured around the sterile room. “Now you're just a woman in a bed.”

Olivia’s lip trembled, just for a second. Then she pulled the covers tighter.

“I still have power.”

Andrew nodded. “Sure. But no one left to protect with it. Or from it.”

A long silence passed.

He stood, walking to the door.

Then paused.

"Olivia," he said, without turning back, "whatever kingdom you're building next… make sure it's not on a graveyard."

She didn't answer. But her eyes followed him all the way out.

***

Theodore lay on his stomach in the quiet dark, breath steady, the weight of the city for once not crushing his spine. Moonlight draped over his bare back, illuminating the cruel road map of scars that danced across his skin like broken memories.

Alessia lay beside him, tracing each mark with slow, reverent fingertips.

She didn't speak at first. The silence between them was sacred.

Then, softly:

"These… these aren't just scars, Theo."

Her voice quivered with restraint.

"They're stories."

Theodore stayed quiet. His fists clenched in the sheets.

Alessia leaned closer, her hand gently resting over a deep ridge near his shoulder blade.

“Who did this to you?”

The room went still.

He swallowed, jaw flexing, eyes staring into the dark.

“My mother,” he said finally. “She didn’t raise a son. She raised a survivor.”

Alessia’s heart fractured.

She pressed her forehead gently to his back, as if she could absorb the pain through touch.

“You’re not her scars,” she whispered. “You’re the reason they healed.”

He turned slowly onto his side to face her.

Her fingers never left his skin.

She smiled softly. “So… what’s the plan for tomorrow, Mr. Almost Mayor?”

Theodore exhaled, grounding himself in her presence.

“We hit the morning radio spots. Then final community visits. I’ll give a closing speech on the courthouse steps.”

Alessia nodded, tracing small circles on his chest.

“You need to own your story. Not hide it. Let them see who you really are.”

He looked into her eyes, vulnerable and steady.

“What if they don’t want that man?”

She cupped his cheek, her voice full of conviction.

“Then they don’t deserve him.”

He kissed her forehead, then her lips.

Slow. Certain.

“Let’s win this,” he murmured.

“Then let’s bury the past with it.”

They lay in silence again, her head resting on his chest, their breaths syncing, heartbeats thudding like war drums softened by love.

And for the first time in years…

Theodore Parker finally slept.

CHAPTER THIRTY-FIVE: THE CITY HOLDS ITS BREATH

Date: September 1, 2004 — Election Day

The sun rose over Duschinni Beach with a tension that felt carved into the concrete itself. The city wasn't just awake. It was *alive*. Vibrating.

Old church bells rang over neighborhoods blanketed with campaign posters. Theodore's face muraled on the west side. Adonis' name scrawled like graffiti on the east.

Poll lines wrapped around buildings. Kids waved little Parker buttons. Old-timers whispered about violence brewing in the air like static.

Theodore sat calm in a small studio downtown, voice low but steady, his truth unfiltered.

"We weren't born into privilege. We were born into pressure. And pressure either cracks you… or makes you unbreakable."

But just before signing off, a call cut through the line—raspy, deep, chilling.

"Theodore Parker... how does it feel knowing your past isn't done with you yet?"

Silence.

The call dropped.

The room felt colder.

***

Adonis slammed back bourbon inside Michelle's penthouse, hands shaking.

His campaign manager read the latest polls—Theodore surging.

Adonis' voice snapped like a whip:

"He's not built for this city. I AM."

Michelle glided over, her voice silk over venom.

"Then show them, Adonis. Show them you're more than your father."

***

At opposing polling stations, Marcus caught sight of two blacked-out sedans idling too long.

He radioed Andrew.

"Eyes up. We're not alone. These aren't just voters."

Andrew agreed, fingers tightening around his radio.

"Feels like we're sitting on dynamite."

***

Backstage at the courthouse, Alessia fixed Theodore's tie, hands lingering.

Her voice low:

"Whatever happens today... you fought like hell for your future. That makes you dangerous in all the right ways."

Theodore stared into her eyes.

"Dangerous isn't what scares me. It's losing you."

She smiled faintly.

"Then don't."

***

On the courthouse steps, thousands roared for him.

Theodore stepped to the mic. Every scar, every demon, standing with him.

"Duschinni Beach... I'm not here because I'm perfect. I'm here because I'm proof that broken things can lead. That wounds don't disqualify you—they prepare you."

The crowd erupted.

***

CRACK!

A single gunshot ripped through the summer air.

Screams.

Chaos.

People ducked. Bodies scattered.

A figure collapsed.

Blood on the concrete.

***

High above, from her private suite, Michelle swirled her wine, eyes never leaving the coverage.

Her whisper was cold enough to shatter glass:

"Right on schedule."

CHAPTER THIRTY-SIX: FALLOUT

Date: September 1, 2004 — Election Day (Later That Day)

Duschinni Beach was chaos wrapped in sirens.

Police barricades snapped up around the courthouse. Helicopters sliced through the sky. News vans swarmed like locusts.

People screamed. Others cried. Some stood frozen, covering their mouths, unable to believe what had just happened.

A single gunshot. A lifetime of consequences.

Alessia was covered in blood.

Not hers.

She didn't even know whose.

She shoved through the panicked crowd, screaming, raw and desperate.

"THEODORE?! THEO!!"

Her heart pounded like it would explode from her chest.

Officers tried to hold her back but she fought like hell.

"Where is he?! Somebody tell me where the hell he is!"

Marcus ducked under crime scene tape, his detective badge glinting in the chaos.

Andrew was already there, his uniform stained, his face pale but locked in.

They didn't need words.

Both of them thinking the same thing:

Please not Theo.

Andrew gritted his teeth, voice shaking.

"We need to secure this whole damn block. Shooter's either long gone or still hunting."

Marcus nodded, cold, dangerous.

"Nobody leaves. Nobody moves until I say so."

Some said they saw him duck into a black car.

Others swore he hit the ground when the shot rang out.

But one thing was clear:

Adonis Perry vanished into the chaos like the wolf he was.

And that made him *even more dangerous*.

***

High above the city in her suite, Michelle sipped from a crystal glass, watching the news unfold like a conductor watching her orchestra burn.

"One bullet," she whispered to herself. "That's all it takes to change history."

Her phone buzzed.

A single message from her inner circle:

"Courthouse secure. Shooter gone. Outcome unknown."

She smiled faintly.

"Activate Plan C. Let them tear each other apart."

***

She dropped to her knees outside the courthouse steps, shaking, the weight of fear crushing her.

Her phone buzzed in her shaking hand.

A message from an unknown number:

"We have him."

Her breath caught.

Her lips parted.

But no name.

No details.

Just those three words.

***

Heaviness loomed over Duschinni Beach.

The city didn't feel alive anymore.

It felt like it was bleeding.

CHAPTER THIRTY-SEVEN: THE WOLF RISES

Date: September 1, 2004 — Late Night

Alessia's nerves were razored thin. Every sound, every flicker of shadow clawed at her fraying sanity. The steering wheel dug into her shaking hands as she tore through the desolate streets toward the docks.

"Warehouse 17. Midnight."

Her pulse thundered in her ears. Sweat slicked her spine. The line between fear and hope blurred until it didn't exist anymore.

Was it Theo waiting for her? Or something darker? Something final?

Every reflection in the rearview mirror felt like it stared back at her.

Every red light felt like blood.

***

Marcus and Andrew tore through files, footage, and street contacts with a surgeon's precision and a wolf's hunger.

"Warehouse 17 keeps popping up," Andrew muttered.

Marcus's stare was sharp, cold. "Feels staged. Feels like bait."

"Then why leave clues? Why make it obvious?" Andrew pressed.

Marcus loaded his weapon. "Because whoever left it wants us to come. Wants us to see something."

Andrew looked uneasy. "Or someone."

Adonis was a storm without mercy.

Street informants avoided him like fire.

"Warehouse 17," one finally whispered, shaking. "That's where all roads end tonight."

Adonis chuckled darkly. "Or begin."

Alessia arrived first, heart hammering in her throat. The docks were dead quiet. Too quiet.

Moments later, Marcus and Andrew arrived, guns drawn, eyes sweeping every shadow.

Then came Adonis, stepping from the night like the darkness birthed him.

Marcus's voice was sharp. "Of course you'd show up. Buzzards always circle blood."

Adonis scoffed, his gaze icy. "Careful, detective. Buzzards eat dead things. You're still breathing... barely."

Andrew cut in with a growl, "Cut the macho crap, both of you. We have one mission tonight—find Theo. We don't have time for pissing contests."

Alessia, her voice shaking but fierce, snapped, "While you two measure egos, he's in there—alone, or worse."

Their bickering ceased instantly. A sound—a distant clatter deeper inside—snapped their attention like a whip crack.

Weapons lifted. Hearts surged.

It was time.

Inside, cryptic messages were scrawled on pillars and walls in sharp, jagged writing:

"How far would you go for truth?"

"Pain builds kings."

"Not lost. Becoming."

Blood droplets marked a trail.

Alessia whispered, terrified, "Theo... what did they do to you?"

Marcus's gut twisted. "No... what did *he* do to himself?"

Chains swung overhead. Their footsteps echoed like the ticking of a bomb.

They reached the center of the warehouse.

Empty.

Except...

A single, rusted chair sat facing away from them.

A figure sat motionless in it.

Bloodied hands resting on his knees.

The figure slowly turned his head, revealing sharp, calm eyes.

A grin that wasn't Theo's.

A voice both familiar and utterly foreign rasped:

"Took you long enough."

CHAPTER THIRTY-EIGHT: THE CROWN'S KISS

Date: September 1, 2004 — Late Night

Charlotte Parker stood in front of her cracked apartment mirror, rouge dusting her cheeks like war paint. Lipstick like dried blood. Cheap pearls strangling her neck.

"Time to shine, Charlotte baby," she whispered to herself, grin twisting. "They all forgot about Mama... but Mama never forgets."

She gathered the store-bought bouquet and left.

The hospital halls stretched forever. Quiet. Late-night graveyard quiet.

Charlotte moved like a ghost dressed in church clothes.

She smiled sweetly at the tired nurse at the desk. "Just five minutes, honey. Woman to woman. We mothers gotta stick together."

They let her in.

Olivia looked like a fallen queen in that bed—bandaged, scowling weakly at the approaching devil.

Charlotte sat down slowly beside her.

"Well, well, well," Charlotte purred, her voice honeyed poison. "Ain't this a sight? Olivia Schumacher, high and mighty, laid out like yesterday's trash. Life sure has a twisted sense of humor."

Olivia's rasp was dry, venomous. "If you came to gloat, you can kiss my ass, Charlotte. I buried bigger threats than you."

Charlotte chuckled low, shaking her head. "Sweetheart, you didn't bury nothin'. You just built your pretty little kingdom on bones like mine. My pain. My story. And didn't even leave me scraps."

She leaned in, voice dropping to a terrifying lullaby.

"But see... a woman like me? I don't stay buried long. No, ma'am. I rise. We old snakes, we shed skin and bite harder."

Olivia's glare weakened but held. "You're pathetic. You're... forgotten."

Charlotte's eyes glinted with madness.

"Oh sugar... forgotten? Honey, I ain't a memory. I'm the storm they never see coming. And tonight... I'm gonna write my own ending."

Her hands slid slowly, lovingly around the pillow.

"And you? You're just... loose ends."

Charlotte's voice grew giddy, almost sing-song.

"Night-night, Liv. Send my love to the devil. Tell him Mama's coming for his throne next."

The pillow dropped.

Olivia's muffled screams clawed at nothing.

Charlotte's face softened into pure, serene satisfaction.

Like rocking a baby to sleep.

Charlotte opened the door slowly, wiping away fake tears with a tissue.

"Nurse! Oh lord, I think... I think she's gone... she... she stopped breathing!"

Chaos erupted.

Charlotte slipped out into the night like a shadow wearing pearls.

She didn't look back. She didn't need to.

Alone in the hospital parking lot, Charlotte lit a cigarette, exhaling slow as the flames reflected in her wild, hungry eyes.

"Time to reclaim the crown, baby. Time for Mama to shine."

CHAPTER THIRTY-NINE: GHOSTS IN THE STREETS

Date: September 2, 2004 — Early Morning

Duschinni Beach woke to breaking news chaos.

TV Screens. Radios. Headlines.

*"Olivia Schumacher Dead in Hospital Room." "Election Postponed Indefinitely Pending Scandal Investigation." "Courthouse Shooter Still Unknown." "Candidates Theodore Parker & Adonis Perry Missing From Public Eye." "Unidentified Body Found Washed Ashore On East Beach. Investigation Ongoing."

***

Alessia, sitting in the hospital's staff lounge, nearly dropped her coffee.

"Olivia's dead? No way... No way."

Nurses around her buzzed like hornets.

"Heart attack? Accident?"

Alessia's gut told her something darker. Her heart whispered one chilling name:

Charlotte.

***

Marcus slammed a fist into his steering wheel.

"We were just there. We were just there!"

Andrew shook his head. "It's too damn convenient. First the courthouse shooting, now Olivia dead in her bed? Feels like chess moves, man."

Marcus stared out the windshield. "Feels like Charlotte Parker got herself back on the board."

Marcus and Andrew began tracking Teddy's growing trail of destruction.

A corrupt landlord found in his office, tied to his chair, belt marks scarred across his face.

A drug dealer hung upside down in an alley, a crude note carved above him:

"Pain Makes Kings."

And then the latest scene—a former dirty cop found bruised, barely alive, taped to a statue of Lady Justice downtown.

Spray painted in blood-red letters across the marble base:

"YOU MADE HIM A MONSTER. NOW I'M HIS SHADOW."

***

In her luxury suite, Michelle sat poised, watching Charlotte's latest tear-filled TV appearance.

Michelle's smirk curled.

"Oh Charlotte, you really think the throne comes without blood?"

She turned to her assistant.

"Set a meeting. I want to see what kind of queen she really is."

Marcus arrived late to another grisly scene.

Blood smeared across the concrete.

A single calling card, more sinister than any before:

"THE FINAL NIGHT WILL BELONG TO THE BROKEN. WAREHOUSE 9. MIDNIGHT."

Marcus stared long and hard, the weight sinking deeper.

"Warehouse 9... That's where legends go to die."

Somewhere in the city, in the dark, Teddy whispered to himself:

"Time to end this. One scar at a time."

CHAPTER FORTY: THE BROKEN BUILD KINGS

Leonard Ashford poured himself aged whiskey in his lavish office—floor-to-ceiling windows overlooking the city he'd carved like a butchered animal.

He never heard the door close.

He never saw the shadow slip in behind him.

Teddy's voice, cold, calm, chilling:

"How many families did you destroy while you sat in this chair, Ashford? How many kids like me lost homes... while you lined your pockets?"

Ashford turned, face draining of color.

"You're Parker's kid..."

Teddy stepped forward, boots leaving silent shadows. "Wrong. I'm what Parker's kid *became*. Because of men like you."

What followed wasn't murder. It was revelation.

Flash drives tossed onto the desk.

Pictures.

Documents.

Proof of every dirty deal Ashford thought buried.

And the wall behind him? Spray-painted in brutal, shaking hands:

"YOU BUILT EMPIRES ON BROKEN CHILDREN."

***

Marcus arrived seconds too late.

Ashford alive—shaking, humiliated, ruined.

Andrew whispered, awed and horrified:

"He ain't hunting victims, Marcus... he's hunting sins."

Marcus clenched his jaw. "He's escalating. Warehouse 9 is next. And I don't think he's stopping until one of us falls."

***

Alessia, standing alone in the quiet of her apartment, whispered through tears:

"Theo... Teddy... please... come back to me. Let me bring you home. Let me reach *him*."

Her phone buzzed.

Unknown number.

One word: *"Come."*

Warehouse 9.

***

Warehouse 9 was deathly silent.

Chains hung like gallows.

Teddy stood in the center. Calm. Back turned.

He spoke without looking:

"You shouldn't have come."

Alessia stepped forward. Her heart threatened to cave in.

Voice shaking. Strong. Bare.

"If I didn’t come... then who would? Who ever came for *you*, Teddy? Who stayed? Who held you when the world turned its back on you and him?"

Silence like a blade.

Teddy's shoulders stiffened.

"You came for the weak part of him. The part that needed saving. I buried that boy. I became what he needed."

Alessia's tears poured now, raw and unguarded.

"No... You didn't bury him. You loved him. You carried him! When no one else would. When *she* broke him. When this city ignored him. You were his shield, Teddy. You are his heart. But he doesn't need to hide behind you anymore... because now he has me. And I swear to you... on my soul... I'll never let him be alone again. Never."

Teddy finally turned.

Eyes sharp. But glassy. Aching.

Voice like a wounded guardian:

"Do you know what it's like to sit in the dark and tell a crying boy he's worth more than every scar his mother gave him? To take every blow, every nightmare, and hold them in your chest just so he could sleep? I didn't ask to be born... I was *made* the night she broke him. And I would do it again. Every damn scar. Every fight. To keep him breathing."

Alessia stepped closer.

"You saved him, Teddy... but let me love him. Let me love *both* of you."

A long pause. The longest of their lives.

Then a crack in Teddy's armor. A tear. Not weakness.

Honor.

He whispered:

"Then love him for everything he is. Even the pieces that look like me."

And then—as if a great weight lifted—he stepped back.

Theodore's breath hitched.

His eyes blinked through the haze.

"Alessia..."

She ran to him, arms wrapping around him like she never wanted to let go.

He whispered against her hair:

"You brought me home. You brought me back."

To himself. To the city. To the ghosts.

"No more hiding. No more running. I am Theodore Parker. And I'm coming for every damn lie this city built. Starting with Charlotte."

CHAPTER FORTY-ONE: BLOOD IN HIS VEINS

Date: September 2, 2004 — Late Night

Adonis stood in his penthouse staring out over Duschinni Beach, his city unraveling beneath him.

Ashford humiliated.

Olivia dead.

Julian missing.

And Teddy? Out there carving a legend in blood and fear.

His phone buzzed.

Text from one of his guys: *"Michelle meeting with Charlotte Parker at The Monarch Lounge. Thought you should know."*

Adonis's jaw tightened until his teeth ached.

"Unbelievable."

Michelle sat perfectly poised in a private lounge, sipping bourbon like a woman with nowhere to rush. Charlotte sat across from her, nervous energy barely contained beneath fake pearls and a plastic smile.

Charlotte preened, half-drunk on her newfound fame.

"I'm finally being seen for who I am... the mother who survived raising that broken boy. The city sees me now. They want my story."

Michelle's smile never wavered.

"Funny thing about stories, Charlotte. They don't always end the way you want. Especially when blood's involved."

Charlotte chuckled nervously. "Blood? Oh please, honey... that boy was the worst thing that ever happened to me. If his father hadn't left me high and dry, I would've been somebody a long time ago."

Michelle leaned in, voice velvet and venom.

"Interesting choice of words... *'his father.'* You sure that's all there is to it? Because I hear secrets have a funny way of crawling out of graves."

Charlotte's smile cracked for the first time.

Adonis stormed into the lounge like thunder walking on two legs.

"What the hell is this?" he barked.

Charlotte visibly jumped, nearly spilling her drink. Michelle, cool as winter, didn't flinch.

"Adonis... sweetheart," Charlotte stammered, standing halfway like she wasn't sure to run or beg. "It's not what it looks like. We were just... talking."

Adonis' stare cut through her. "Talking about what? You? Riding my family's coattails now? Trying to cash in again? You're like a damn roach, Charlotte. Always showing up when the lights go out."

Charlotte fumbled, voice shaking. "I-I've been through hell, Adonis! Raising a boy like Theodore... you don't know what that does to a woman!"

Michelle snorted softly into her glass.

Adonis' lip curled. "Oh, I know what bad mothers look like. Lived with one long enough in spirit."

Michelle set her glass down, slow, deliberate.

"But what if you're not just looking at a bad mother... but *your* mother, Adonis?"

Charlotte went pale as ash.

"Michelle, you shut your damn mouth—"

Adonis turned on Charlotte like a predator scenting blood.

"What. Did. She. Mean."

Charlotte's hands fluttered like dead butterflies.

"Listen, baby... sweetheart, it was complicated... I-I was young, Julian was powerful, things happened... I signed papers... they told me to forget—"

Adonis roared, fury splitting through his control.

"Forget WHAT, Charlotte? That you left me? That you buried me like I was garbage? That I've been at war with my own bloodline and didn't even KNOW IT?"

Charlotte whispered, shaking. "I didn't have a choice..."

Michelle, watching with the calm of a queen playing her final card, added with a vicious smirk:

"Funny thing about choices, Charlotte... you always had them. You just never chose love."

Charlotte broke then.

Full collapse.

Adonis stood over her like a storm reborn in human skin.

Later, alone in Julian's abandoned office, Adonis tore through drawers with silent fury.

He found it.

Old photo.

Hospital document.

Julian's hand-written note: *"A mistake I could never erase. A son I could never claim."*

Adonis exhaled like a man seeing his own ghost.

Adonis, whispering to himself, eyes burning like the city outside his window:

"Blood never lies... but neither do scars. And I'm about to leave plenty."

CHAPTER FORTY-TWO: PILLOW TALK — A WORKING THEORY

Date: September 3, 2004 — Early Morning

The Duschinni Beach Coroner's Office was colder than usual. Marcus Cain's boots echoed on the polished concrete as he pushed open the double doors. The sterile air carried that sharp chemical tang of antiseptic and death.

Dr. Eric Rowe, the Medical Examiner, was scribbling notes under the flicker of fluorescent lights.

"Morning, Doc," Marcus said, voice gravel-low.

Rowe barely looked up. "Cain. You're here early. Autopsy results came in late last night on Schumacher. Figured you'd be here soon enough."

Rowe led him to a steel table where Olivia's file sat.

"Burn patterns? Minimal. Shrapnel wounds? Superficial. None of them were fatal," Rowe began, his voice clinical.

He tapped a page. "Primary cause of death: asphyxiation. Smothered. Most likely with a pillow or soft object. Note the petechial hemorrhaging around the eyes and the slight compression bruising across the nose and mouth."

Marcus leaned in. His mind was already calculating.

"Smothered in a hospital bed during chaos," Marcus murmured. "Bold... but desperate."

Rowe nodded slowly. "Whoever did it was close. Intimate. Not a hit. Not random."

Marcus's mind clicked hard. A predator didn't smother a powerful woman in a hospital unless it was personal... or calculated.

Pillow Talk. A working theory was born.

Rowe hesitated before speaking again. "Got something else you might want to see. Pulled in a John Doe from East Beach early this morning. Male, 50s-60s. Suited. No ID. But..."

He slid a small evidence bag across the table.

Inside? A distinct signet ring.

Marcus's stomach turned to lead.

Julian Perry's family crest.

Marcus masked the shock behind deadpan eyes.

"Prints?"

"Running 'em now," Rowe replied. "But you and I both know who we're probably looking at."

Rowe led Marcus to the cooler. Drawer 9.

Marcus pulled it open slowly. The bloated features were unrecognizable to most.

But not to Marcus.

The sharp jawline beneath swelling.

The old scar behind the left ear—from a knife fight back in '84 Marcus had read about.

Marcus whispered under his breath:

"Julian Perry..."

Marcus stepped back, rubbing his jaw.

Two storms were brewing:

- Charlotte Parker had motive, opportunity, and just enough stupidity to leave evidence behind.
- Julian Perry was dead... and Adonis didn't know.

And Marcus? Smack in the middle of both infernos.

Marcus, walking into the night, jaw clenched, his detective instincts sharper than ever:

"Pillow Talk... let’s see how loud Charlotte screams when I knock on her door."

CHAPTER FORTY-THREE: UNRAVELING THREADS

Charlotte Parker adjusted her blouse and smiled sweetly into the handheld mirror. She was being prepped for a late-afternoon segment with a local news station—her second appearance this week.

"They want the raw truth," she told the makeup artist. "That's what sells. And I gave this city pain wrapped in pearls. I survived Theodore Parker. That boy nearly destroyed me, and now look—I'm finally being heard."

She had no idea that Marcus Cain had already connected her scent to the edge of a hospital pillow.

She had no idea that every step she took toward the light brought the shadows closer.

***

Marcus leaned against the nurse station in Duschinni General, flashing a badge but speaking in low tones.

"Off the record," he told Nurse Ellyn. "You remember anything odd the night Olivia Schumacher died? Visitors? Anyone who shouldn't have been near the room?"

Ellyn looked around and lowered her voice. "There was a woman. Said she was a friend. Older, overdressed. Red lipstick and this fake air of elegance..."

Marcus's pen stopped mid-note.

"She said she was Olivia's sorority sister. But Olivia went to college out of state... we looked it up later."

Marcus murmured to himself, "Charlotte Parker... 'sorority sister,' huh?"

A thread tugged. He pulled it.

***

Adonis sat in the campaign war room surrounded by silence and shattered glass. The large television was off. Phones muted. A whiskey bottle half-drained sat near the edge of the conference table.

Michelle stood nearby, arms crossed, stone-faced.

"You're unraveling," she said coldly.

Adonis didn't even look up. "He's turned the entire city into a funeral procession. For me. For Olivia. For Julian."

Michelle snapped. "Then be a leader! Rebuild the damn strategy! We had them cornered!"

Adonis looked up slowly, eyes bloodshot and haunted.

"We had power. Teddy took fear. He made the city believe he's the reckoning they never saw coming."

Michelle flinched at the name. "He's one man."

Adonis stood, glass shattering underfoot.

"He was one man. Now he's a damn symbol. And symbols don't bleed."

News reports whispered about exposure and corruption. Teddy had dropped files from Leonard Ashford's system into the public domain. Names, dates, bribery logs. All authenticated.

The Michelle-Adonis campaign machine? Paralyzed.

Donors fled.

Public support wavered.

The people whispered:

"Maybe Parker's the purge we need."

Theodore himself remained silent.

But the city spoke louder every day in his place.

Back at his desk, Marcus pulled up Charlotte Parker's visitor log.

She signed in as "Rebecca Sloan."

He exhaled slowly. Pulled up Charlotte's DMV record.

The handwriting was a match.

Marcus leaned back, his stare unreadable.

"Almost got away with it, Charlotte. Almost."

***

In her apartment, Charlotte sipped champagne, rehearsing her next monologue in the mirror.

"They'll never forget me. I'm a survivor. The mother of the most talked-about man in the city."

Outside, a storm cloud darkened the glass.

And still... she didn't see it coming.

CHAPTER FORTY-FOUR: LEGACY UNBORN

The bathroom light was unforgiving. Alessia gripped the porcelain edge of the sink, knuckles white as she tried to steady herself.

Another wave of nausea hit. Violent. Unrelenting.

She heaved again. Dry. Her stomach a hollow drum, her chest tightening like her body itself was holding something sacred hostage.

Her long dark hair clung to her damp face, strands sticking like threads of reality unraveling. She pressed her forehead to the cool glass of the mirror. Her reflection didn't even look like her.

Pale.

Haunted.

Empty-eyed but full of something else.

Stress. It's the stress. Or the lack of sleep. Or...

Her eyes drifted—fearful, unready—to the unopened pregnancy test box on the counter.

That small rectangular box might as well have been a loaded gun.

A soft knock jolted her.

"Les?" Rhea's concerned voice. "You okay in there? You've been in there a while. You're scaring me."

Alessia forced her voice steady—but even that wavered.

"I'm fine, Rhea... bad sushi. I swear."

Even the lie burned her throat on the way out.

But the truth?

The truth terrified her more.

Marcus Cain's apartment was a battlefield of evidence.

Papers everywhere. Visitor logs. Surveillance stills. DMV records. Fingerprint analysis. Every thread weaving tighter like a noose around Charlotte Parker's painted throat.

He zeroed in on the name scrawled in cheap blue ink:

Rebecca Sloan.

"Cute alias, Charlotte... real cute."

He flipped through the visitor log images and circled one faint, greasy smudge left behind.

A fingerprint.

"Sloppy."

Marcus grabbed his phone and punched in Rowe's number.

"Eric. Cain. I need those latent prints processed yesterday—match it against DMV records for Charlotte Parker. Cross-check handwriting samples while you're at it."

Rowe grunted. "You're not letting this go."

"Not a chance."

He leaned back, exhaling slowly.

"This ain't just murder... it's pride. And Charlotte's about to drown in it."

The back of Adonis's black SUV was silent save for the sound of glass rattling against glass.

His grip on the whiskey tumbler was tight enough to crack it.

His mind was unraveling.

Charlotte's betrayal.

Michelle's calculations.

Julian's disappearance.

And the name echoing like a curse in his skull:

Teddy.

His father's voice haunted him:

"You're a weapon, Adonis. But weapons rust when you stop fighting like you mean it."

The whisper on the streets hit him harder than any fist ever could:

"Maybe Parker's the one we needed all along..."

Adonis muttered like a dying prayer:

"I'm not done... I'm not done... I'm not done..."

But deep down?

He felt it.

He was bleeding.

And the city smelled it.

That night, Alessia sat on the edge of her bed.

Everything around her was quiet except for her racing heartbeat.

The pregnancy test box was now open. The stick in her hand. Timer on her phone ticking like a time bomb.

She squeezed her eyes shut, fighting the tremble in her body.

Theodore... Teddy... me... are we enough? Are we ready for this?

Seconds crawled.

Minutes mocked her.

Beep. Beep. Beep.

She dared to look.

Positive.

Her breath shattered.

Her hands covered her mouth as her eyes blurred with tears.

Joy.

Fear.

Love.

Dread.

A life was inside her.

Not just any life.

The legacy of Theodore Parker.

Her whisper broke into the dark like the gentlest thunder:

"Oh my God... Theodore... I love you. I love you so much."

Voice shaking, heart splintered open, she whispered into the quiet:

"If this is real... everything changes. And so do we."

CHAPTER FORTY-FIVE: THE COMPANY YOU KEEP

Theodore and Andrew walked the polished halls of Duschinni General Hospital. Andrew, still healing but running his mouth like nothing happened, strutted alongside Theodore like he owned the place.

"I'm tellin' you right now, Teddy," Andrew grinned, "soon as I'm cleared for duty, I'm gettin' me one of these little carts to ride around the city. The 'Andrew Express.' No lights. No siren. Just vibes."

Theodore chuckled under his breath. "You would crash that thing in thirty minutes flat. Probably flirtin' with a nurse while drivin'."

Andrew clutched his chest dramatically. "Sir. How dare you? I am a professional paramedic and a hopeless romantic. I multitask with grace."

They turned a corner—and froze.

Michelle Winslow-Perry.

Elegant. Cold. Alone. Stepping out of the OBGYN office.

Pamphlets on first-time motherhood peeking from her designer tote.

A momentary pause.

Andrew blinked. "Ain't no way that's..."

Theodore's jaw tensed. Eyes narrowed. "Oh, it's her."

Michelle caught their stare.

If she was rattled, she didn't show it. Instead, she smoothed her hair, adjusted her sunglasses, and offered a thin, venomous smile.

"Parker," she said like greeting a distant enemy.

Theodore nodded slightly. "Winslow."

Michelle stepped closer, voice silky.

"Seems we both have surprises brewing. Life's funny that way. The trick is surviving them."

Andrew mumbled, mostly to himself, "Bruh... ain't nobody ready for this soap opera."

Michelle's eyes flicked to Andrew, a slow smirk tugging at her lips before she strolled away like royalty leaving peasants behind.

Silence stretched between Theodore and Andrew until Andrew finally broke it.

"Bro... listen... that baby? That could be Julian's. Not Adonis's. You know that, right? Old man was still out here actin' brand new."

Theodore exhaled slowly, watching Michelle disappear down the hall.

"Timing is too perfect. Julian disappears. Michelle glides in pregnant? In the middle of an election war?"

Andrew shook his head like it hurt to even say. "Man... if that's Adonis's brother or sister she carryin'... that's game over. That boy gon' lose his mind."

Theodore's voice dropped, dangerous and low.

"Or become exactly what Julian always wanted. A monster with nothing left to lose."

Andrew clapped Theodore on the shoulder. "You know what, Teddy? Ain't no love story in this city clean.

Everybody got dirt under their fingernails. But Michelle? She's plantin' landmines in the dirt. And we just stepped into the field."

Theodore nodded slowly, never looking away from the OBGYN door.

"Then we better watch where we walk. And who we walk with."

Theodore, quiet, calculating, staring down a war he didn't start but damn sure planned to finish:

"This city ain't about blood anymore... it's about legacy. And legacies kill more than bullets ever will."

CHAPTER FORTY-SIX: THE POISON WE DRINK

Flashback: The Night of Seduction

Dark.

Luxury apartment.

Glass of imported whiskey swirling in Adonis's hand.

The taste?

Smoother than usual.

Or was that just the haze settling over him?

Michelle Winslow-Perry straddled him slowly, moving like silk over skin, her lips brushing his ear, her perfume heady, intoxicating.

Michelle (whisper-soft): *"Let it go tonight, Adonis. Let legacy write itself."*

His body relaxed. His mind fogged. Her hips rolled slow and deliberate.

He blinked.

Her voice echoed again, darker:

"Men die every day, Adonis. But legends... legends leave something behind."

Darkness swallowed him whole.

Present Day: The Interview That Set The City On Fire

Morning television.

Michelle—flawless.

Wrapped in pearl-white elegance. Subtle baby bump barely noticeable under designer couture.

Reporter leaned in, hungry for blood.

Reporter: *"Michelle, the city's swirling with rumors. Are you confirming the pregnancy?"*

Michelle smiled that slow, deadly smile.

Michelle: *"I don't confirm rumors, darling. I create history."*

Boom. The room gasped. The city shook.

Reporter (pressing): *"Is Adonis Perry the father?"*

Michelle's pause was art.

Michelle (faint chuckle): *"I believe legacies are built over decades... not declared overnight. Some men leave behind wealth. Others... leave something a little more permanent."*

Gasoline.

Fire.

The internet exploded.

Julian Perry's name trended like a ghost rising from the grave.

His grip shattered the remote in his hand.

The glass cracked like his restraint.

Adonis (muttering): *"She set me up... that night... that drink..."

The camera had cut away just as Michelle's eyes slid toward the lens like a silent challenge *just for him*.

***

Evening.

Adonis entered their private estate—silent. Measured.

Michelle sat outside on the patio, sipping tea as if empires weren't burning around them.

He sat across from her.

Adonis (low, lethal): *"That night. What was in the drink?"*

Michelle's lips curled, soft, devastating.

Michelle: *"Hope. Control. Power. And maybe... a little future insurance."*

Adonis's jaw flexed.

Adonis: *"Is the child mine? Or is it Julian's?"*

Michelle laughed under her breath—like knives scraping silk.

Michelle: *"You poor thing... always so eager to claim what's yours... yet terrified to raise what might not be."*

Slice.

Michelle: *"Do you think legacy is about blood? Ask Julian. He bled plenty. And look where it got him."*

Slice.

Michelle: *"But you, Adonis... you think a last name makes you a king? No. It makes you a target."*

Slice.

Michelle (leaning in, voice razor-thin): *"The real question isn't who fathered this child... it's who survives raising it."*

Adonis stood—silent, shaking with a rage that couldn't find release.

Michelle (final cut, low and sweet): *"Congratulations, Adonis... you're already a father. To paranoia, fear, and a city that wants your head on a platter. And the baby? The baby belongs to whoever wins this war."*

Adonis stormed away, but her whisper chased him like the devil itself:

"And I always bet on me..."

CHAPTER FORTY-SEVEN: THE DAY BEFORE EVERYTHING CHANGES

Charlotte Parker sat in her modest apartment, basking in the warped glow of local fame. The champagne was cheap, but tonight it tasted like royalty.

Until the knock came.

Slow. Measured. Final.

Marcus Cain entered with the look of a man dragging the past behind him.

"Charlotte Parker," Marcus began, laying the folders down like a coroner placing a body tag, "you done left fingerprints on everything except your conscience."

Her smile cracked slightly.

He laid down visitor logs, fingerprint analysis, pillow fibers, and finally—the hospital footage.

Charlotte's voice barely whispered, "You're here to arrest me?"

Marcus stared, hard. "No. I'm here to show you how damn loud silence gets when a guilty woman runs outta lies."

She laughed—small, bitter.

"Tell Teddy... I raised him alone. I raised him hard. But I never raised him for this world."

She stood, excusing herself to the bathroom.

But Marcus felt it.

Too calm.

Too final.

Seconds later— the sound of breaking glass.

He rushed in.

Charlotte lay slumped, crimson blooming from a self-inflicted wound beneath her chin. The mirror shattered. Her life finally still.

But her hand?

Clutching an envelope.

On it: *"For Theodore."*

Meanwhile, Alessia sat in her office at Duschinni General Hospital, scanning the hospital's network. Her mind ran a thousand miles, restless over the storm brewing everywhere.

An unaddressed encrypted file caught her eye.

"CONFIDENTIAL: EYES ONLY. OPERATION: WINSLOW FALCON."

She opened it slowly.

Coordinates.

A meeting time.

A note: *"Protect the Asset. Even From Herself."*

Her blood ran cold.

In the corner of the screen: An ID code she hadn't seen in years.

Her father's.

Matthew Tolliver.

Quiet. Loving. *CIA.*

Always told her politics was dirtier than war.

She whispered to herself:

"Dad... what the hell have you been doing?"

***

Adonis paced backstage at the election rally, sharp-dressed and coiled like a weapon ready to fire.

Michelle's interview replayed in his mind like a ticking bomb.

His speech sat in his hands.

Lines of vengeance.

Lines of legacy.

Lines about *Teddy*.

But then—

Every screen in the venue blared alive.

BREAKING NEWS.

"Authorities have now confirmed the body found on East Beach is that of local mogul JULIAN PERRY. Suspected foul play. Investigation ongoing."

The crowd gasped.

Adonis stood frozen.

Eyes wide.

Julian.

Dead.

His father.

Gone.

A legacy in flames.

Across the city, Theodore Parker watched the coverage with Andrew by his side.

The silence between them cut deeper than words.

Andrew muttered, "The King is dead... and tomorrow, we see who’s left standing."

Theodore's jaw clenched.

"Tomorrow... isn't about kings. It's about the future. And some legacies? They start in blood. But they end with choice."

Adonis stepped to the podium, heart hollowed out.

He stared at the screaming crowd, the city holding its breath.

"Let me tell you about legacies..."

CHAPTER FORTY-EIGHT: THE ATOMIC REVEAL

The phone buzzed on the table like it already knew the weight of the call.

Unknown Number.

"Mr. Parker... we need you to come down to Duschinni General Hospital. It's... regarding a matter that requires your personal identification."

No name given.

But in his gut? Theodore already knew.

Alessia placed a shaking hand on his shoulder. "You don't have to go alone."

He turned, with a hollow echo in his voice. "Yes... I do."

Marcus stood like a stone pillar by the stainless steel table.

The air reeked of sterile finality.

"She left this for you," Marcus said quietly, handing over the envelope.

Without a word, the sheet pulled back.

Charlotte Parker.

The monster of his youth.

Now? Small. Fragile. Powerless.

Teddy's presence behind Theodore felt... still. Not gone. Watching. Weighing.

Theodore took the letter with hands steadier than he thought possible.

"Theo,

If you're reading this... then I've done what I never could do in life. I've shut up.I raised you in the fire because that's all I ever knew. I wanted you hard because I was terrified you'd turn out soft like your father... or lost like me. But the truth is... I was jealous. You survived me. Hell... you became something I never could. I can't ask forgiveness. I wouldn't believe I deserve it even if you offered. But if you're standing, if you're breathing, if you're reading this... you're already stronger than every demon that raised you. Burn this city if you have to. But live. Really live. Your mother, for better or worse, Charlotte."

Remote safehouse.

Matthew Tolliver.

Sharper than any father had the right to be.

Files laid out like weapons.

"Michelle Winslow-Perry," he began, "isn't just the most dangerous woman in Duschinni Beach. She's a ghost from the CIA's darkest black books. Operator. Assassin. Asset gone rogue. Your city? She's been using it like a chessboard since before you could vote."

Alessia's voice cracked. "Dad... it was you, wasn't it? You shot Theodore... to save us."

Matthew's stare cut deeper than any bullet.

"If I hadn't... you'd both be dead. Michelle had plans that night. Fatal ones. I had to do what I do best... protect my own."

Tears blurred Alessia's vision.

She stepped closer, her voice shaking but filled with life.

"Well, Dad... you didn't just save us. You saved your grandchild too."

Matthew's hardened expression fractured.

His voice dropped, raw.

"Grandchild...?"

Alessia nodded, wiping away tears.

"I'm pregnant, Dad. You're going to be a grandpa."

For the first time in years, Matthew Tolliver's breath caught.

Not in strategy.

Not in calculation.

But in the fragile wonder of life he thought he'd never touch again.

Breaking News.

JULIAN PERRY CONFIRMED DEAD.

Adonis stood on stage, shoulders trembling.

The crowd silent.

He leaned into the mic, venom personified.

"Let me tell you about legacies..."

Pause.

"My father built a kingdom of lies. And maybe the cruelest of all... was building sons he never planned to keep."

Another pause.

"Michelle... my own stepmother... could be carrying my brother... or worse... my father's last spit in my face."

GASP.

Chaos erupted.

Cameras exploded in flashes.

Adonis, almost laughing through rage:

"Blood means NOTHING in this city. Legacy? It’s carved by whoever survives the storm."

***

Theodore, staring at Charlotte's letter.

Alessia rushing in, clutching the file that could drown Michelle forever.

Their eyes met.

Shared understanding.

Shared war.

Teddy's shadow leaning in the background.

Theodore spoke low, like thunder before lightning.

"Tomorrow... the city learns... blood might start legacies..."

His eyes cut razor sharp.

"But truth ends them."

CHAPTER FORTY-NINE: THE BIRTH OF TRUTH

The city roared outside. But here? In the quiet hallway backstage?

Theodore stood alone. Wrestling ghosts. Wrestling history.

Until Alessia appeared. She didn't run to him—she walked like gravity itself pulled her closer.

She stopped inches from him. No crowd. No press. No noise.

Only them.

Her hand trembled on his chest. But her voice?

Steady.

"Theo... I need to tell you something before you walk out there."

His eyes searched hers, instinctively bracing.

"I'm pregnant."

Silence.

But not emptiness.

The world fell away—like the universe held its breath.

Theodore blinked. For a man who had been crushed by life, this moment... felt impossible.

He laughed under his breath, raw, cracking with emotion.

"You're pregnant? With me? With this mess of a man?"

She nodded, tears brimming.

"With you. Exactly you."

Then it came out of him like blood finally leaving a wound that never closed.

"Alessia... I love you. I love you so much, it's stupid. I love you like breathing hurts without you near."

Her sob broke the vacuum.

She kissed him, desperate. Fierce. Home.

"Win or lose tonight, Theodore... you are everything right in my world."

The crowd was electric.

Adonis stood before them—not a man anymore, but a fuse.

"Duschinni Beach... you were built by men like my father... destroyed by men like my father... and now? You're watching the last of his sins bleed out on this stage."

Eyes everywhere.

Media breathless.

"Parker... if you think blood makes you ready for this city... you don't know what this city is. It's a predator. And it chews up boys like you."

Pause.

"But I hope you prove me wrong. I dare you."

Theodore's Revolutionary Speech

The walk from backstage to the podium felt like walking into the lion's mouth.

Theodore gripped the edges of the podium. Looked over the sea of faces.

And smiled.

No fear.

No politician.

Just a man.

"I'm not supposed to be here."

The crowd shifted.

"I'm not polished. I'm not perfect. Hell, I'm barely put together most days. But I'm still standing."

He looked at Adonis, dead in the eyes.

"Not because my bloodline gave me strength... but because surviving hell gave me clarity."

"Duschinni Beach doesn't need a king. It doesn't need a tyrant. It needs people willing to tell the truth when it costs them everything."

He paused, scanning the crowd.

"I am not here to sell you hope. I'm here to fight like hell for it. For every forgotten street. Every child left in the cracks. Every scar that's become armor."

"I'm Theodore Parker. Son of nobody's dream. Fighter of every nightmare."

"And if you'll have me... I'm yours."

Silence.

Then—like thunder cracking over water—the city erupted.

CHAPTER FIFTY: KINGS, CROWNS, AND QUIET WARS

It wasn't just a scandal.

It was annihilation.

News outlets across Duschinni Beach exploded with revelations of Michelle Winslow-Perry's crimes. Her black-ops history leaked like a virus into every home. Project Vesper Fox wasn't just a file—it was a death sentence.

Footage rolled of offshore accounts, weapons trafficking, political blackmail. Anonymous sources flooded the media. Marcus and Matthew Tolliver operated in the background like war generals.

Michelle's arrest wasn't quiet. Federal agents paraded her down the front steps of her empire in handcuffs. Protesters chanted. Graffiti on the gates read:

"WITCH OF WINSLOW"

Marcus watched from his car window, a small grin curling on his face.

"Just like the old days," he muttered.

The city buzzed. News loops chronicled everything.

- Olivia's calculated rise.
- Maribel's tragic death.
- Adonis Perry's fiery warpath.
- Theodore Parker's raw revolution.
- Michelle's collapse.

Duschinni Beach was battered. Bruised. But breathing anew.

"And now... the moment Duschinni Beach has been waiting for... the announcement of your next mayor..."

The coverage continued... but we wouldn't hear it yet.

***

Location: Alessia's Family Backyard

The sun bathed the setting in gold.

A large white banner fluttered overhead:

"CONGRATULATIONS!"

A double-meaning. A beautiful ambiguity.

Theodore and Alessia stood surrounded by love and life.

Marcus manned the grill, hollering at Andrew.

"Boy, don't make me tell that story about you passing out in your EMT test!"

Andrew fired back.

"Only if I can tell the one about you crying at Titanic, tough guy!"

Laughter rolled over the yard.

Alessia's parents hugged her. Maribel's parents brought handmade gifts. It felt... pure. Earned.

Matthew Tolliver stood at the fringe, ever the protector, a ghost softened by family.

Little kids played tag around Theodore's legs.

Andrew handed Theodore a tiny onesie:

"Future Mayor's Assistant. Pay: Unlimited Juice Boxes."

Election coverage continued.

"...And the new mayor of Duschinni Beach is—"

Location: High-Rise Penthouse. Empty. Cold.

Adonis sat in silence.

TV playing low behind him.

The ring of Julian Perry—the Crescent King—in his hand.

He stared at it for a long moment.

Then slid it onto his finger.

Slow. Deliberate.

Not surrender.

Coronation.

A whisper:

"Long live the king."

Dark. Dangerous. Eternal.

Theodore kissed Alessia's temple as family surrounded them.

Love. Legacy. Life.

The TV played behind them...

"......And the new mayor of Duschinni Beach is—"

To be continued......

EPILOGUE

Duschinni Beach, Florida
Late Night

The city looked peaceful from a distance.

Streetlights reflected against rain-soaked pavement while ocean waves rolled calmly against the shoreline. Downtown buildings glowed beneath the humid Florida night like nothing bad had ever happened there.

Like the city itself had no memory.

But cities remembered everything.

Especially cities built on secrets.

Inside a dark office overlooking the water, a television flickered silently against the wall. News coverage replayed fragments of the recent chaos gripping Duschinni Beach. Politicians smiled through rehearsed statements. Reporters talked about recovery. Stability. Unity.

Lies wrapped in expensive suits.

A man sat alone in the shadows watching it all unfold.

Still.

Silent.

Patient.

A glass of bourbon rested untouched beside him.

Another lightning flash illuminated the office windows for half a second, briefly revealing old photographs scattered across the desk. Names. Faces. Bloodlines.

The foundations beneath the city.

The real history no one was supposed to uncover.

The man leaned forward slowly, studying one particular photograph longer than the others.

Two infant boys.

Same birthday.

Different destinies.

His expression never changed.

Outside, thunder rolled over the ocean.

The storm had passed.

But something worse was coming.

The man finally reached for a folder resting near the edge of the desk. Black ink stamped across the front read:

PROJECT: BLOODLINE

CLASSIFIED

He opened it carefully.

Then smiled.

Far below the office tower, Duschinni Beach continued breathing through the darkness, unaware that its real war had only just begun.

www.ingramcontent.com/pod-product-compliance
Ingram Content Group UK Ltd.
Pitfield, Milton Keynes, MK11 3LW, UK
UKHW041635190726
13854UKWH00006B/2500

9 798234 074454